I0775360

# The Crèche Keepers' Guild

Ware Wilkins and Faith Anthony

Published by Vintage Pixie Press, 2023.

*Copyright © 2023, Vintage Pixie Press*
All rights reserved. No part of this book may be reproduced or used in any manner without the prior written permission of the copyright owner, except for the use of brief quotations in a book review.

# Table of Contents

*For Joel and Bill*

*To: The Babysitters' Guild*

*The Temple of Dinna respectfully requests two new members for the role of temple crèche teacher for six children. Must be certified in basic safety and child-management. Experience preferred, but exceptions will be made for the right applicant. Must be willing to cook and assist in basic maintenance of the crèche area. Competitive pay commensurate with experience level.*

*Kindest Regards,*

*Pearl, Acolyte of the Goddess, Temple of Dinna*

*To: The Babysitters' Guild*

*I am once again requesting two teachers for our temple crèche. I sent a message several days ago, but perhaps it was lost? I know we have developed a bit of a reputation, but I'm sure your members are more than capable of caring for a few mischievous children. If pay is an issue I am happy to negotiate as the temple elders allow, but please keep in mind that we are the temple of a minor goddess, and our pockets are not as deep as those with more prominent patrons. I look forward to meeting whoever you deem suitable for the position.*

*Kindest Regards,*
*Pearl, Acolyte of the Goddess, Temple of Dinna*

*To: The Babysitters' Guild*

*Please, I'm begging you. I know one of the children set our last teacher's robes on fire, but I assure you that was an accident. We're happy to accept anyone you want to send. Literally anyone. Maybe an apprentice? I ardently await your reply.*

*Kindest Regards,*

*Pearl, Acolyte of the Goddess and very very tired, Temple of Dinna*

# Chapter One

The little bastard's sleep sack was gone.

Anah surveyed their camp, disbelief ransacking her brain. Hailee, still snoring in her bag, remained unaware of the betrayal that had occurred while they slept.

Fear clutched at her as Anah went to the pack where they stored their loot. The thick sounds of the jungle coming alive surrounded her as she peeked inside. It was still there, so maybe Bucket hadn't—

But he had. The bag was picked over. A single pouch remained that jingled when she shook it and at least had some heft. Because Bucket liked tricks, though, she checked the contents. He'd left them the gold. Anah imagined Bucket viewed it as some sort of conciliatory prize. Shaking, she checked her bag as well, needing to see that the relic, the item she'd been dreaming about for years, was still there. She tore through her stuff. The relic wasn't there.

The relic they'd all ventured through icy mountains, dangerous caverns, and a mega buttload of kobolds to get.

Bucket had taken it and run. The little halfling jerk.

"What's cooking?" Hailee grumbled, rolling up to a seated position. "Oh. It's you."

Anah pressed fingertips to her temples and rubbed circles while she counted to ten. Inside, the coal of anger had become an inferno. As a fell-touched cambion, losing her temper wasn't an option—not if they didn't want to spend their morning putting out fires. It took a few deep breaths to stop her skin from smoldering.

"You woke up pissed." Hailee was poking at their campfire, trying to breathe life back into it. Anah pointed a finger and sent a blue burst of flame straight into the coals. "Thanks, boss." Hailee set to rummaging in the pack of foodstuffs.

"Have you noticed anything *askew* with our campsite?" Anah ground out. She, Hailee, and Bucket had been a crew for several years, and yet Anah still managed to be surprised with the monk's complete inability to sense when something was wrong. Well, no, that wasn't right. Hailee maintained an undeserved optimism that things would always work out for the best, so her instinct for danger was more than muffled. Ordinarily, this lack of insight wasn't something you'd want to see in a crewmember, but what Hailee lacked in common sense she made up for with an easy-going nature and fists of absolute fury.

"I mean, I noticed a complete lack of brekkie." Hailee grimaced at whatever she was seeing in the food pack. "I'm starving."

"Nothing else? Nothing missing?"

With an irritated huff, Hailee looked around. Twice. Anah felt her skin prickling with heat again and was about to erupt when her companion cursed. "Bucket?"

"Bucket," Anah agreed. "Gone. Along with the jewels and the relic."

"That little bastard!" Hailee was up then, picking through the loot pack just as Anah had. She held up the coin purse. "Dummy forgot the money, though."

"I don't think he did." Anah stood and began to pack up, her movements quick and economical. "I think he views it as... paying us off. A 'please don't come after me and pull my small and feeble body parts off' sort of gesture."

Anah didn't add that her anger at the desertion wasn't solely tied to the loot. Yes, they were adventurers and mercenaries—an occupation not known for loyalty or reliability. But one couldn't dodge death with folks without growing fond of them. She'd thought Bucket was a friend. He was sneaky and conniving and could pick just about any pocket, but he was also good company. They'd spent countless nights in conversation by the campfire. Bucket and Hailee were the only two people Anah felt understood her, and were certainly the only people she'd allowed close.

While she hadn't specifically told Bucket how important the relic was to her, it wasn't out of secrecy. She hadn't seen the point. Anah couldn't have predicted that he'd pull a stunt like this. The betrayal set her skin to smoking once more.

Seeing Anah, Hailee began to kick dirt over their campfire, eyeing it wistfully. While the jungle was wet and lush, it wasn't fireproof, and they were experienced enough in safety and covering their tracks. "Is that what we'll do? Take the money and walk away? It was only a small cache, really."

Hailee had never asked about the relic, either. She was, Anah mused, an easy companion. Feed her, show her something to punch, and all was well. That, too, was nice to have in a crewmember and friend. Though now Anah found herself wanting to prioritize loyalty above all else. Being funny meant nothing if someone was willing to knife you in the back.

"That relic was important," Anah managed. None of this was Hailee's fault and Anah didn't want to take her anger out on the wrong person. "It's worth far more than even the halfling could know."

The Wand of Birramos was a relic that, once she took it to a fell-stone sanctuary to hone the gem, would allow her access to limitless magic. Being half human kept Anah from using the infernal magic of her demon side without consequence. There was a substantial amount of power, to be sure, but it was a keg that could be tapped and drained. With the wand, though? Her power would be a bottomless well. No more headaches, no more rest periods, no more fell water.

No more crutches or weakness.

"It was a chunk of petrified wood with an uncut ruby in it. If you really want something like that so badly, I'm sure we can use some of this money to craft our own."

Anah clenched and unfurled her fingers, over and over, wishing she hadn't played her cards so close to her chest. But she wasn't in the habit of discussing her weaknesses with anyone, not even friends. "It's a powerful wand, Hailee. One that would have made it easy for us to become the most in-demand mercenaries Deladrin has ever seen."

"Oh. Cool."

"We won't accept his pity pouch. We will one hundred percent hunt that halfling down, get the wand and loot, and teach him that double-crossing us wasn't a good idea."

Hailee seemed to absorb this before she shrugged and hoisted her travel sack over a shoulder. "Yeah, fine. Could I please have something to eat, though?" This was punctuated by a rumble. It was Hailee's stomach, demanding attention.

Anah fought the smile that insisted on coming and failed. "Sure. I've got some dried fruit in my pack. Will that work for now? We've got some tracking to do."

SEVERAL DAYS AND MANY minor spells later, they latched on to their quarry. Halflings didn't garner a lot of attention and Bucket, in particular, was notoriously good at blending in and disappearing. That, in fact, was the skill set that had earned him a place in their team. But Anah was fell-touched and able to cast a variety of spells, not bound to any particular school of magic. Plus, she'd kept a bit of Bucket's hair as an insurance policy against situations like the one they found themselves in. Said hair was now ash, used in a tracking spell.

"He's in Farrow," Anah announced, waving away the lingering smoke from her casting.

"Not too far," Hailee mused. "We can be there before dusk, but it'll be tricky finding him in a city."

Though the trees were large and the verdant overgrowth of jungle threatened to encroach on the cobbled road, travel would be quick. The humidity would be the only thing that might hinder them.

"I'm determined," Anah answered, already starting east. Farrow was a waypoint, the kind of small city right at the cusp of... well, everything. It was the hub adventurers used to restock, to find new jobs, and to sell any treasures accumulated on the road. It was, in short, a place that offered Bucket far too many opportunities to elude them.

They reached the city just as the sky edged from orange to pink. Slipping through carts carrying goods in and out, Anah headed straight for The Drunken Goat. Being a favorite inn of theirs, it was as good a starting place as any. At this point, she was desperate for something solid and familiar so Bucket's betrayal didn't have total command over her headspace.

It was clean inside, the candles already lit in advance of the night. A few patrons sat around over bowls of stew and pints of ale, but the mood was quiet. Anah appreciated it. She'd used quite a bit of magic over the past few weeks and the spell work was beginning to take its toll. A dull pain throbbed behind her left eye.

"Ayo, ladies!" Marcus, the barkeep, waved enthusiastically when he saw them.

Anah's face remained grim, but Hailee dropped her packs so she could go and clap the man on the shoulder. Unlike Anah, Hailee tended to make friends wherever they went. After the two finished an elaborate handshake Anah couldn't follow without rolling her eyes, Marcus looked around the room, his gaze tracing the floor. "Where's Bucket?"

"I was hoping you could tell me that," Anah said as she slid onto a barstool.

The barkeep studied her carefully. "Looks like the bugger got on your bad side." Marcus filled two pints and placed them in front of Anah and Hailee.

"Yeah, he screwed up big time," Hailee said before draining half her drink in one go.

"He didn't pass through here?" Anah dragged her fingertip along the top of her mug, eyeing Marcus's face for any tells.

"Not that I saw," Marcus replied. "Though he can be easy to miss, if you know what I'm saying."

A tiny pang pierced Anah. She was shorter than average, minimizing any attention-commanding aspects her horns might have. Many times on the road, she and Bucket had talked at length about the pros and cons of being small. It had been nice to be seen in that regard. Something Hailee, with her towering height and muscular build, wouldn't be able to understand.

"He's talented like that."

"And he's mega small," Hailee added. It came out mumbled as her mouth was full of bread, so it sounded like "Anth heath mega sthmall". When had the food come? It was then Anah spotted Marcus's wife, Frida, busking about behind the bar. She was as efficient as Marcus was exuberant and most likely the keystone to the Drunken Goat's success.

"Rightly so." Marcus chuckled, but looked Anah dead in the eye and solemnly added, "He didn't stop here. I swear it."

This news only mildly deflated Anah. She hadn't truly expected Bucket to come to the same inn they frequented when passing through Farrow. It had been a hope, but not one grounded in reality. "I don't suppose you have a room for us?"

"That I can help you with." Marcus began polishing mugs.

"My thanks." Anah took a dainty sip of beer, forcing her mouth to unpucker as soon as the sour slick of it hit her tongue. She'd never cared for ale, but it was cheap and besides, she didn't want to be rude.

"And could I get some food?" Hailee had already demolished the bread Frida had brought. A few crumbs stood out against her brown skin, hovering next to her mouth. Without thinking, Anah reached up and brushed the crumbs away. Hailee smiled. "Thanks, boss."

Anah wrinkled her nose. "Please. I just don't want to be followed around by a giant baby who can't get all her food into her mouth. Appearances are important, Hailee." She was teasing and added a grin to ensure Hailee understood, but for a split-second, Anah wondered if she could still make light with anyone. Trust was a scarce commodity and Bucket had just raided her vault.

How long until Hailee left as well?

Soup arrived, thick and brown and smelling like heaven. Far better than the beer, that was for certain. Despite the season's heat and oppressive humidity, there was something basic and comforting about a bowl of soup. While Hailee slurped and joked around with Marcus, Anah retreated into her head and began to plan. She needed about a week's worth of sleep and a draft of fell water to fully recover the magic she'd expended over the past week. Neither would be available until she found Bucket and retrieved the relic. A very which came first, the dragon or the egg situation.

A tiny pool of magic remained in her reservoir. Anah's head throbbed a smidge louder as she considered how to use it. To cast another spell or two would leave her with a piercing headache, but to skip it might allow Bucket a chance to elude them.

Decided, she finished half her beer. The bubbles made her stomach over-full and uncomfortable. She pushed the remainder in the cup over to Hailee. "Tonight, sleep. Tomorrow, we hunt."

# Chapter Two

The market was crowded. Anah cursed under her breath as she followed the magical tug of the spell. Her head pounded and the din of the people milling all around did little to help. Hailee hovered at Anah's side, using her strong frame to help clear a path.

Normally Anah would stop to enjoy the smells of the market. The spice stall, in particular, was a favorite. She had a deep love for all things intensely spicy and the vendor was one of the few who managed to carry goods that lent food a delightful, fiendish burn. Today, however, she was wholly focused on the seeking spell.

It had taken more magic than she wished and the very last of Bucket's hair. Like the first location spell she'd cast, the tracking magic was attuned to the clever halfling. This one homed in on the halfling and required a constant trickle of magic to maintain. Heat flared in her blood. Between that and the sun's insistent caress, Anah was sweating through her linen shirt.

A sharp tug had them turning round a corner. Anah's pace picked up, and she fought back a smile. They were drawing nearer. *He'll wish he never took from me.*

The spell grew insistent. "We're close!"

They followed the pull of it up some stone stairs. Two large, ornate, wooden doors loomed at the top, shut tight. Potted ferns sat on either side and the stone was meticulously swept.

Anah stopped for a moment, taking in the building. It was a temple to one of the lesser gods Dinna. Dinna was the goddess of growth and change. Neither held much interest for Anah. Change was rarely for the better and she'd learned to tolerate the life of the petite. Who needed growth, anyway? The spell yanked, though, and so Dinna's temple it was.

"He's inside."

"Of the temple?" Hailee sounded curious, reaching a finger out to trace the carvings in the door.

"Bucket always had a thing for Dinna, if I remember correctly." Not that religion came up often between the three of them, but spend enough time with a person and their interests will slip out.

Hailee's nose scrunched. "Oh, right. Do you remember how he used to make that joke? About taking his gold pieces to Dinna to ask for change?"

There was a pang in Anah's chest, like a small dagger managing to slide home in her heart. The joke was terrible but it had made her snort every time the rogue had told it. Her spell wavered for a moment and Anah snapped back to focus. "I'm thinking there might be more to that joke than we thought."

Anah debated the next step. Whatever choice she made regarding the last of her magic would be what helped them snare the rogue or aid in his escape. "I'm going to use this last bit of his essence to trap him in the temple," she finally said.

"It's a large enough temple," Hailee mused. Anah knew what she was thinking—large spaces favored their small and elusive friend.

Anah acknowledged the trickiness of the situation. "We'll have to find a way to gain entrance. But he won't be able to leave, so worst-case scenario, I'll take a few weeks to recharge or he'll beg us to let him out." She didn't want to wait a few weeks, however. Anah wanted the Wand of Birramos *now*. She was so tired of being overlooked and misjudged.

"Yeah, okay." Hailee trailed a finger along the etchings in the wood. "Do you need anything from me?"

Anah did. She sent Hailee out for a few components she needed for the ritual to fully seal off all temple exits for Bucket and Bucket alone. She didn't want to deal with the metaphorical headache of angry acolytes and pissed patrons while also fending off a literal migraine due to magic depletion.

When Hailee returned, Anah got right to it. She used charcoal to draw the circle of binding she'd need. To this, she added ground dragon scales to increase the square footage of the spell. There was also a pinch of dandelion for magical longevity, the final hair from Bucket, and three drops of her blood to strengthen the spell.

Infernal words tumbled softly from her lips. Anah's body lit from within, a coal fanned into flames. If any bystander looked at her, they'd have assumed something nefarious was going on. Why else would a fell-touched be casting on the steps of a goddess?

She didn't have to worry, though. Hailee was busy putting on a martial arts show several feet away, the monk's prowess and gymnastics skills demanding the attention of any passersby.

Anah felt the moment the spell took hold like a brisk breeze punching through her and dousing her flames. Her shirt was stuck fast to her skin and her red hair hung in damp hunks. The throbbing in her skull blossomed with the promise of many hours of punishment.

"Okay," Anah rasped. "It's done. He won't be able to leave until the spell runs out or I let him, and the spell isn't running out any time soon."

"Cool." Hailee jogged up the stairs, helped Anah up, and kicked away the evidence of their plan. "Inside?"

"Inside."

Hailee frowned. Her arm muscles corded as she hauled open one of the heavy doors. It squeaked ominously.

They stepped inside. Windows along the top allowed the daylight to pour in, flooding a cavernous room of white marble and green moss. The effect of both was cooling. In the center was a bubbling fountain, surrounded by several acolytes in robes. Pilgrims knelt in alcoves, heads bent as they prayed to the goddess.

"Huh." Hailee pointed. "Pretty deity."

Anah studied a large stone carving of the goddess. Her lip curled at the statue. Dinna looked so... so... *wholesome.* Long hair was shown cascading down soft shoulders and a dress that didn't do much to disguise a generous figure. It was conventionally attractive, Anah thought, but she didn't like the smile carved into the stone face.

It looked less like a warm welcome and more like a mischievous smirk.

"Let's start looking," she said. "Try to be subtle."

"No, duh," Hailee said. "It's a temple." Anah realized she hadn't needed to warn Hailee—after all, her friend had grown up in a monastery as well, honing her body in honor of Nym, a god of sunlight.

They moved quietly, peeking into the alcoves and earning several irritated glares. They circled the fountain. Anah's frustration grew. The inside of the temple was large, but other than the nooks for prayer, there was nowhere to hide. Everything was exposed and the pristine white marble made shadows work hard to exist.

The main hall was a fraction of the temple. It was also the only place general patrons were allowed. That wouldn't stop someone like Bucket, who managed to find ways into the trickiest of spaces, but it posed a challenge for the women. They couldn't go exploring willy-nilly without attracting unwanted attention.

"How are we going to get into the inner sanctums and rooms?" Hailee whispered, tracking several doors that were most likely locked and definitely not for just anyone to pass through.

Anah chewed on her lip as she considered. If she had more in the tank, she might be able to make them invisible, but that was a heavily draining spell and she didn't have enough to make it work for even a second. "We could pretend to be cleaners, maybe? Or pest control?"

As deep in the jungle as Farrow was, pest control was a high-demand job. Insects and rodents were everywhere and they were *gross*.

"Did you see the state of the front entrance?" Hailee asked before gesturing around the high-ceilinged room. "And in here? They already have someone for that, because I haven't seen a single six-legged being yet."

A crash came from behind another set of doors, snagging Anah's attention immediately. "There," she said, rushing over. Her plan was already seeming flimsy. It wasn't just a matter of how to gain entrance, but how long she could tolerate being inside Dinna's home. The temple made her skin itch, like it was a bit too tight.

She'd just grabbed the knob when another bang came, followed by some muffled curses and, Anah could have sworn, some giggles. Hailee's hands became fists and she shifted her feet into a ready stance.

The door was yanked open and both Anah and Hailee jumped back. Anah was prepared to call on her last defense and Hailee's fists were up as they faced—

An acolyte who appeared just as startled as they were. The woman looked to be near their age—late twenties—and was draped in the long brown robes of Dinna's worshippers. Red-faced and flustered, she raised her hands in surrender. "Oh!" was all the woman managed to squeak out.

The risk gone, Anah swiftly tucked her attempt at magic back in, the spike of pain in her head a hefty reminder of how depleted she was. When Anah glanced at her companion, she was startled to find Hailee slack-jawed and moon-eyed.

Hailee stared at the acolyte in mute but utter adoration.

Anah snorted. Of *course* Hailee would find a crush now, when time was of the essence. Choosing to ignore her dumbstruck friend, Anah held out a hand. "Hello and sorry about that. I'm Anah."

The woman's eyes remained wide as she shook Anah's hand. Before Anah could explain—well, lie about—what they were doing, the acolyte said, "Are you here for the... positions?"

That gave Anah pause. Positions?

Another scream and the sound of something heavy toppling over erupted from behind the woman, but Anah couldn't see past her. What she did notice, however, were the wards around the door's frame. Small but pungent with sealing magic. Meant to keep people out? Or things... in?

"Yes." It was Hailee who spoke. Anah inhaled sharply. What was she doing? "We're here for the positions."

The fighting stance was gone, and Hailee was standing straight as a board, pink blooming in her cheeks. Anah swallowed down a groan. Then again, this was exactly the kind of thing they'd been searching for.

She just hated not knowing what it was.

The woman looked them over once more, taking in the canvas pants and linen shirts, the road-worn boots still caked in dirt. Her gaze brushed over Hailee's well-muscled body before lingering on Anah's horns. Anah bit the inside of her cheek. Though there were a few fell-touched in Deladrin, that didn't mean acceptance always came easily.

Some people couldn't get over a little demon in one's heritage.

"You're sure?" the woman asked, and no, Anah wasn't sure, but it didn't matter because Hailee was already enthusiastically agreeing like a puppy in search of belly rubs.

"Thank the goddess." Anah didn't like the amount of relief the woman's words held. What had Hailee just volunteered them for? "Follow me."

Anah watched with interest as the woman made several quick signs with her hands. This was followed by a minute flash of the wards. With that, she turned and started off. Anah and Hailee followed.

The room they entered seemed to be used for storage. Though it was hard to tell as several pots lay in pieces on the floor. Further, there were dustings of powder here and there, peppered with tiny footprints.

*Aha!* The footprints were definitely Bucket-sized. They must be in the right place. Perhaps the positions were for tracking insolent halfling thieves hiding out within the temple walls. Doubtful, but Anah tried to remain optimistic that they could do what they needed to and get the hell out.

The woman crossed through another door, forcing Anah to leave behind the prints. This new room was a kitchen with a monstrous hearth and several large tables covered in assorted copper pots and pans. A stack of used pewter plates and cups were sitting next to the wash bin, waiting to be cleaned. The woman ignored them. It was here she stopped again and faced them.

"I'm so glad you're here. I've been reaching out to the guild for months and had begun to suspect they're avoiding me. My name is Pearl."

Pearl's voice would have been soft and bell-like if not for the constant strain that gripped each word.

"Me too," Hailee said, eyes too dreamy for comfort.

Anah suppressed a sigh. Hailee's quick thinking, lust-driven or not, had brought them to this inner sanctum. This was exactly the kind of access they'd needed, but Anah was wary of just what they were signing up for. What guild was Pearl referring to?

There were a variety of guilds in Farrow. Aside from the numerous adventurer hubs, there were the masons, the potters, the merchants, the drivers, and hundreds more. Anah could narrow it down a lot if she assumed a temple didn't need something like, say, the alchemist's guild, but the truth was, Anah didn't know much about temple workings. Or what temples might need.

She realized Pearl had been saying something and none of it had registered.

"Pardon?"

"I was saying we've been running a skeleton crew for far too long. Farrow has a surplus of mercenaries, adventurers, cults, and guilds, but not a lot of people willing to help out in our temple."

Anah bit back the hundreds of retorts that hovered on the tip of her tongue, especially considering that was what she'd just been worried about. Concern over just what kind of help they had been roped into was mounting quickly, but she managed a version of truth. "I believe it."

"I've been stretched thin, having to cover every role alone. I'm sure you can imagine how well that's gone. Desperate as I am, I hope you don't mind answering a few questions?"

"It can't hurt," Anah asked, hoping that was true. It would be nice if Pearl would drop even a hint about what she needed.

The acolyte appraised them again before asking, "How are you under stress?"

"We've been in more than our fair share of stressful situations, and Hailee and I rely on each other to keep calm heads and figure our way through." Anah worked hard to stay honest while not giving anything away. Plenty of adventures had put them in tight spots, yet here they were, bluffing their way through a mystery interview.

Anah considered mentioning she found situations like this, where understanding social cues were critical, far more stressful than, say, a river of acid.

"Good." Pearl nodded, pinching her chin thoughtfully. "What about difficult personalities? How are you with those?"

Hailee chuckled. "Anah's the most difficult person I know and we've worked together for years. We can manage." Anah shot her companion a look that promised retribution, but Hailee was too busy beaming at Pearl.

"Years?" Pearl appeared to be impressed, which only added to Anah's wariness. Stress? Difficult personalities? So far exactly zero things regarding this prospect enticed her. "It sounds like you have a lot of experience."

They did, heaps and heaps of it... but Anah didn't think adventuring and mercenary work was what the acolyte was referring to.

A muffled shriek came from somewhere beyond the kitchen, and Pearl blanched, her put-together mask dropping. Her eyes flooded with panic, forcing Anah to reconsider. Maybe skilled adventurers were exactly what they needed. "I wish I could give you a more proper interview, but for now I'll have to trust the wards."

That caught Anah's attention. "Wards?"

"You saw them on the door. They only let through those seeking Dinna's help."

Anah was caught off guard. She found Hailee staring at her, features slack with surprise. They were here for a jerk of a halfling only. If the goddess wished to assist in that, well, great. But Anah suspected if Pearl was as worn down as she said, the wards probably weren't up to par. Gods knew Anah couldn't have placed wards worth anything until she recovered. Most likely they weren't a blip on the goddess's plan. Anah preferred to keep it that way.

"Well, I suppose we'll see how the goddess works," she ventured.

Pearl's eyes momentarily narrowed. "Yes. Today will be a trial period. I'll be keeping an eye out. If we agree you should stay on, it'll be four silver bits a week."

Four silver bits wasn't bad for a job. But Anah, Hailee, and Bucket had cleared triple that amount when the right scores came along. Remembering their trio brought another surge of anger. Why had Bucket decided to run? What had been so bad about their group? Or was it not the group, but just Anah who was the problem?

"That sounds fair." Anah wasn't planning on staying. She'd retrieve the gems and, more importantly, the Wand of Birramos, and then it would be as much gold in a week as she wished with the jobs they could score. The sheer power she'd get from the relic once it was repaired...

She would finally be seen for what she was, horns or no horns.

"Great. This way." Pearl turned, and Anah could see what had Hailee crushing so hard. Pearl's hair was the kind of long and shiny that spoke of regular washings and care, not long stretches on the road. Skin that didn't spend weeks under the sun. And curves similar to the goddess's whose temple they walked through.

Hailee had always been a sucker for curves. Anah ... found the occasional person charming enough for a light round of flirtation. But beyond that? Maybe it was her fell blood, but she was quite... meh about intimate relationships. Besides, she had all the connection she needed with her crew. At least, she'd had it before Bucket had abandoned them.

Bucket was one of two people who'd managed to earn her trust, and where had that got her? In a freaking temple, accepting a mystery job, with no magic left in her tank and no Wand of Birramos.

Pearl led them down some stairs. At the bottom was a door, and the noises from behind it could only be described as chaos. Anah's body ached as she tried to scratch up some defensive magic. There wasn't any to be found. She glanced at Hailee, grateful her martial friend was there.

The door swung open. The cacophony ceased.

"Settle down, please." Pearl was moving and Anah and Hailee had no choice but to follow. Only, Anah discovered a deep desire to run as soon as they entered.

*Oh no.*

# Chapter Three

The walls were painted the sunshine yellow of nightmares. Primary colors screamed from a multitude of surfaces—surfaces like tables and chairs that were far too small for adults. Art was stuck to the walls, scribbles and nonsensical imagery that Anah couldn't begin to interpret.

Small blocks, pillows, cubbies... and the smell of sour milk.

There, seated on a woven mat in the center of the room, were children.

"Aww," Hailee said, giving the kids a wave. Not one waved back. They did, however, stare daggers at the newcomers.

Anah's blood began to ice. This couldn't be what she thought it was. There was no way she and Hailee, seasoned mercenaries, had been roped into *this*.

"Children," Pearl said, spreading her hands, "these are your new teachers." She gestured to Hailee. "This is Hailee. And next to her is Anah."

Hailee being addressed and introduced first was usually a thorn in Anah's side. It irked her to no end that people continually insisted that size corresponded to respect. This time, however, she wished her name hadn't even been mentioned.

Several pairs of eyes locked onto her. Anah saw a gnome, his face covered with soot and his smile devious. He was dwarfed by the two young orcs next to him. Twins, Anah realized, their colored shirts the only discernible difference between the two. There was an ornwas as well, her cat-face relaxed as she flexed her claws as if checking for mess. Anah observed the tiny, needle-like tips and shuddered. A young human girl with a crust of yellow snot under her nose stared absently. And a boy who looked to be part... dragon? Her heart skipped a beat. She'd never seen a dragonling in person.

"There are two of them," Pearl continued, "which means you'll have constant care."

It came out sounding like more of a threat than Anah was comfortable with. She was not used to this kind of security detail.

"Now, I have some work I've put off for far too long. I'll let your new teachers take over from here."

Frozen, Anah remained mute as Pearl sauntered back. Just before she left, she tapped at a slate hanging beside the door. "Here's the schedule. Please stick to it. Other than that, all I ask is that they stay alive and out of trouble."

"That seems like a low bar," Hailee whispered. Anah couldn't help but agree, yet did low mean easy?

The door shut behind the acolyte.

Anah and Hailee swiveled around slowly to face the children. Together, they'd faced off against werewolves, vampires, kobolds, and more. So why in the eight hells did these children scare her so much?

"Hello," she ventured, nerves crackling worse than the time she'd faced down a group of trolls. "I'm Anah."

"You have horns," the little human girl said, mouth slack. Her blonde hair was in pigtails that sort of mimicked horns.

"You're kidding," Anah replied in a dry tone. Her horns were large, curved, and the first thing anyone noticed about her.

"Not kidding. Look at them!" A tiny human finger pointed. The young gnome snickered.

Before Anah could say something sharp, a cheerful "and I'm Hailee!" came from her friend, who dared to appear excited about their predicament. Anah had so many questions and no time to ask them. If Bucket were there, he'd be on her wavelength.

*Bucket is here somewhere and I need to find him.*

First things first, though. No matter the job, the first thing to do was take control of the situation. In this case, Anah understood she'd have to fake it until she made it—made it out of the temple doors with her treasure, that was. "Let's hear all your names." Anah met the small gnome's gaze. There was something mischievous in those eyes that she didn't trust one bit. "You first."

"Call me Snoop Dug." He crossed his arms over his chest and smirked.

"Is that your name? Or just something you thought was clever?"

The smirk faltered a little before moving back into place. "It's my name. Snoop is the family name and Dug because I come from the Underhill gnomes."

*You should go back to the Underhill gnomes and be obnoxious there.*

"And you?" The twins shifted under her scrutiny. The one wearing an ochre shirt rasped out "I'm Bruiser." Next to him, in blue, the other orc child squeaked out, "I'm Stump!"

Hailee stifled a snort that Anah understood. They'd come across quite a few orcs in their travels and their traditional names could be... interesting. "Bruiser and Stump are good, strong names," her companion managed. Based on their large, bulky bodies, Anah imagined Hailee was right. In a few years' time, they'd be absolute giants.

However, the twins looked at each other like they weren't entirely sure what was going on. *Hopefully, their brains grow with their bodies.*

"And you?" She pointed to the cat-girl with tawny fur.

Fluffy ears twitched and green eyes blinked slowly. "Cheese."

"Your name is not cheese," Anah said, tone flat. This was quickly becoming ridiculous.

"Is so."

Snoop Dug let loose a maniacal giggle that raised goosebumps on Anah's arms. "Her name is Eve but we all call her Cheese."

Anah raised an eyebrow. "Why do you call her that?"

The cat girl moved in a languid stretch. "That's easy. Because I love cheese." Those green eyes grew soft and dreamy. "I love it so, so much."

"But it makes you toot," the young human complained. "It's really terrible." This she said to Anah, like it was imperative she understand that under no circumstance was Cheese to eat, well, cheese.

"I can't help being lactose intolerant," Cheese whined. "Something so delicious shouldn't make people's tummies hurt so much."

"Moving on." Anah shifted to the small, snotty human who was still staring warily at Cheese. "Who are you?"

"I'm Hope. I love rainbows and kittens and one time my dad brought me back a kitten from his adventures and it was the sweetest kitten and she was all spotty and had a pink nose and whiskers that tickled me and I called her Ruby because Ruby is a good cat name don't you think? But then one day Ruby escaped the house because I forgot to close the door and then my dad had to go on another job and brought me here and sometimes I get so worried about Ruby because what if she comes home and I'm not there and dad's not there and she doesn't know where to look for me here at the temple?"

Anah took an inadvertent breath as if she'd spoken that monster of a tangent instead of Hope. "I'm... sorry?"

"Yeah, that's sad about poor Ruby. But I bet you'll go home and she'll be there and everything will be just fine." Hailee squatted and patted the girl's head.

"Don't say that," Snoop scolded. "It's no good getting hopes up when you can't be sure of the outcome. Besides, not everyone has a home to return to." There was venom in his voice, but Anah caught another, more familiar tone stitched through the words. Heartache. He wasn't talking about Ruby.

A flicker of something like empathy rippled through her. It was unwanted. Yes, she knew what it was like to fear hope. Control was always better. That was something the young gnome would understand more deeply as he got older—preferably without her aid..

She was itching to run. But the spell had locked Bucket inside and so inside she had to remain.

"You're right. Hope"—Anah almost couldn't with the sheer irony of the girl's name—"sorry about your cat. But you're here now, and so are we, so we're all just going to have to make the best of this situation."

The small girl cocked her head, and Anah had a moment of blood-chilling anticipation of tears, but then Hope shrugged and sat.

That, Anah supposed, was a narrowly dodged disaster. Wait, who was she kidding? This day was turning into an absolute catastrophe. How had one feckless halfling led her into a freaking babysitting gig?

There only remained the dragonling. It was the first time in Anah's life she'd seen a dragonling in person. Bipedal, humanoid, but covered in a sheen of green-blue scales. They had yellow eyes with black slit pupils, which gazed lazily at Hailee. The snout ended in large, round nostrils that twitched as though being tickled.

"This is Stevie." Snoop Dug introduced the dragonling with a pat on their shoulder. "They're getting over a cold."

It was difficult for Anah to reconcile the startling, lizard-like features of the dragonling with the name "Stevie."

"Okay," she said, trying to reassert herself as someone in control. It wasn't clear whether she was trying to convince the children or herself. "Well, there we go. Introductions have been made. What comes next?"

Hailee leaned over and whispered, "I think we're the ones who're supposed to decide that."

Anah pinched the bridge of her nose before remembering that Pearl had mentioned a schedule. She walked over to read it.

Morning: breakfast, reading, play.

Afternoon: Lunch, rest, chores.

Late Afternoon: Parent Pick Up.

How was that remotely helpful?

"So... reading?" Anah asked, not liking the tentative quality of her tone. She was the adult, damn it.

"We already did our reading," Snoop replied with a twinkle in his eye. "Now it's time for *play*."

# Chapter Four

Tiny spiders seemed to be crawling up Anah's skin. "Okay, so go play." This was punctuated with a fluttering of her hands at the open spaces of the room. "Frolic. Make believe. Whatever it is you do."

The children burst into action, whooping loudly and clambering over each other as they rushed around. Anah slid up to Hailee.

"So, how exactly do you picture this working?"

"I mean, the schedule's right there, Anah. I imagine we'll play a bit, then eat lunch, then the kids can take a nap."

Anah tried not to scream. It was like the entire situation kept shifting as soon as she got the chance to try and regain her footing. "I meant about *Bucket*. How in the hells are we supposed to find him if we're trapped watching over these kids?"

Hailee scrunched her nose. "We'll be here. We can take the kids on like... expeditions maybe? Under the guise of exploring the temple?"

"That's a good idea, Hailee." Surprise painted her words.

Hailee beamed. "Maybe we can stick around and help Pearl after as well." This time it was evident Hailee wasn't thinking about finding Bucket.

Anah shook her head firmly. "Don't bother. We're not here for the long haul."

Hailee pouted. Anah knew she'd get over it in the next city with the next pretty woman Hailee stumbled across. But to get there, they needed to finish this job.

"Do you want to get them together and we'll begin?" Anah was already trying to categorize and plan so they could use the children the most efficiently—while having to deal with them as little as possible.

Hailee's grin faltered. "Pearl might not like that. Not on our first day. She said she was going to observe us. If we go out now, we'll probably blow our cover."

Was her companion actually enjoying all this? Still, Anah couldn't fault her logic. So far their attempts to find Bucket had been a bust. How much could children be trusted, anyway? And her magic reserves were beyond tapped. "Fine."

Hailee didn't wait before rushing over to Stump and Bruiser, who were currently wrapping swaths of fabric around each other in a semblance of dress-up. Anah let out a heavy sigh and went to sit in one of the tiny chairs. The fact that it wasn't too small rankled her.

Hope sidled up to her, pointer finger comfortably resting up one nostril. Anah swallowed down bile. "What do you want?"

"I want to play."

Anah leaned back. Was this a trick? "So go play."

"I want to play with you." The finger moved inside the nostril. Anah was going to puke if she pulled out a booger.

"No."

Off to the side, Bruiser, Stump and Hailee were having a pseudo wrestling match, where Hailee looked to be the only one having fun. The two half-orcs kept stealing longing looks at the bin filled with cloth. Anah scanned the room and found Stevie at a large piece of slate with chalk, drawing scribbles. Cheese and Snoop Dug were huddled in another corner, surrounded by blocks.

And Hope was still standing next to her, picking her nose. "Go play with one of the other kids."

The little girl shook her head. "Usually Teacher makes us play a game together. I want to play with you."

Anah bit back what she wanted to say, which was something along the lines of she'd rather have both of her legs ripped off by an ogre and eaten in front of her than play with Hope, and instead managed an "I see."

"We could play hide and seek."

Anah considered it. The room they were in was far too small for such a game, but perhaps it would give her an opportunity to scout around for Bucket.

Hailee popped into her mind and loathe as Anah was to admit it, her companion was right. Until they had a better understanding of the temple and she had recovered some magic, this awful job was their best opportunity to access Bucket's hiding spot.

And the wand.

If Anah had just taken better care of the wand, none of this would have happened. The gem wasn't functional yet, needing the fell jeweler, but the potential it provided was enough to make Anah giddy. No more depleted magic stores. No more people speaking to Hailee first, assuming Anah was a child because of her size. Or worse, not speaking to her because she was a fell-born cambion.

Bucket lifting it off them was just another toxic reminder that Anah was rarely taken seriously. Apparently not even by a so-called friend. Like this child, where her *no* seemed to have zero sticking power

"What about dolls? We could play dolls."

"Do I look like someone who plays dolls?"

Hope considered this, dragging her dull eyes up and down Anah's body before resting once more on her horns. "Yes," she replied with finality. "Anyone can play with dolls."

"I don't play with dolls." Anah felt her patience fraying to the point of breakage.

The finger finally withdrew from its nostril perch, coated in glistening snot. *Grossgrossgrossgross.* "We could play—"

"I've got a headache. No playing." Anah rubbed at her temples to sell this point. Her head was actually throbbing and if no didn't work, perhaps this would.

Hope squinted. "Are you going to die?"

"Yes."

The little girl's mouth dropped in horror, and her little lower lip began to tremble. Anah groaned to herself before launching into an explanation—she didn't want to deal with tears on top of everything else. "I mean that everyone dies eventually, Hope. I'll die, Hailee will, Pearl, Snoop Dug, the twins... even you. We're all headed toward death all the time."

Instead of comforting the child, Anah's words seemed to escalate the situation like fey fire. "I'm going to *die*?"

"Not at this exact moment—"

"I don't want to die! I don't want you to die!" Small hands—one with a still snot-slicked finger—began to reach for Anah, seeking comfort. She leaned away.

"Neither of us is going to die right now. I'm talking big picture stuff here, kid," she insisted. "Hope, I just have a headache. That's all. I've used a lot of magic over the past few weeks and now I'm dealing with the side effects, okay?"

This managed to cut through the oncoming meltdown. Hope's eyes went wide. "You do magic?"

"Yeah."

"Can you do some now?"

Anah inhaled sharply and held the breath before releasing it slowly. "No. I just told you I've used too much magic and it's given me a massive headache. Could you *please* go play?"

"Maybe your head hurts because of a tumor." Hope stared at her, sage-like expression on her face. "A tumor could make your head hurt."

"Seven hells, it's not a tumor!"

For a moment, it looked like Hope was going to dig her heels in and try to diagnose Anah despite having been told the source of the headache. The exchange was exacerbating the pain to an unfair degree.

"We could play beauty parlor. I could make your horns look pretty with ribbons and stuff."

Anah snorted her frustration out her nose like a bull before saying, "I've got a game we can play." Hope's face lit up. "It's called Duck, Duck, Go Screw Yourself."

While Hope was saying "I don't know the rules to that game", Hailee was bounding over waving her hands and saying

"Okaaaaay," clearly desperate to run interference before Hope discovered just how magical Anah could be.

"Cool." Hailee shot Anah a look of warning which frankly felt unfair before putting her hands gently on Hope's shoulders. The little girl reached up and patted them. Anah decided not to tell Hailee about the snot finger. "So the twins aren't feeling wrestling, maybe we can—"

A small series of sneezes interrupted Hailee's proposal. Hope ducked down, covering her head with her hands. The twins pushed over a table and hid behind it as the sneezing grew in intensity.

It was Stevie. A cloud of chalk surrounded the dragonling's head. The next sneeze brought forth a small lick of flame.

"What in the hells—" Anah started before another sneeze elicited an actual spout of flame.

The table closest to Stevie was singed. The slate seemed to shimmer with the heat. The dragonling's eyes watered, their snout wrinkled, and Anah and Hailee had just enough time to hit the floor before a gut-doubling sneeze ripped through the dragonling.

Heat scorched along Anah's back, and when she dared to look up, the dress-up box was on fire. "Hailee," she ordered, pointing. Her companion was up and moving, fluid and determined. Hailee stamped out the small fire.

Smoke had filled the room. The twins and Hope were coughing. Anah, fell- touched as she was, closed the distance to Stevie. She grabbed the bottom hem of their shirt and held it up over their nose to filter out the chalk cloud. Paying close attention to their body, she guided them away from the slate and toward the door. "Keep this here," she told Stevie, pointing to the impromptu shirt mask.

Anah opened the door. Her eyes stung from the smoke and she waved it out of the classroom. It took painfully long minutes to diffuse the room enough that the children stopped coughing. Hailee carried the box of charred dress-up remains into the hallway.

Heart pounding from adrenaline, Anah leaned back against the wall.

"No more chalk today, Stevie."

The dragonling lowered the shirt to expose a sheepish smile. Some cold part of her threatened to thaw in that moment, but before Anah was too at risk of feeling something good, her sixth sense for trouble began to thrum.

"Something's wrong here."

Brow furrowed, she scanned the room. Yes, it was still smokey, but not overmuch. The table and the dress-up box were the only items that showed any damage from the sneeze attack. Hope, Bruiser, and Stump were already making jokes amongst themselves.

Nothing stood out until—

"Hailee?"

"Yeah, Boss?"

"Where are Cheese and Snoop Dug?"

# Chapter Five

The kitchen was empty, much to Snoop's delight. Miss Pearl might be only one woman, but she was one woman who seemed to always know when he wanted to stray from the rules.

Not like the two new teachers. If you could even call them that. Anah and Hailee had blundered into the classroom like stupefied cows and it had taken Snoop approximately two seconds to start listing possibilities for ways to take advantage of their naivete. Honestly, if Miss Pearl wasn't stretched so thin, she'd never have let those two dunderheads into the temple to begin with.

Guilt slicked through him momentarily. None of the teachers Miss Pearl found stuck around long.

It was possible he had something to do with that. Snoop couldn't help that, so far, the Childcare Guild had sent terrible hires.

"I'm going to the ice box," Cheese said as she cheerfully skipped over to the thick clay box used to keep perishable items cool. "I think I saw some yogurt there earlier."

"Just promise not to put your cot next to mine at rest time."

Cheese's farts were impressive, but no one in their right mind would want to be stuck next to them for long. Snoop did enjoy imagining how that fell-born, Anah, would handle the stench. She was the first fell-touched person he'd seen and it would have been interesting if her face wasn't constantly pinched.

The other one, Hailee, didn't seem so bad. But he suspected she was almost as much a kid as he was.

"What are you going to do?" Cheese asked, already sweeping a finger through an open container.

"Dabble is all."

Snoop wasn't an inherently "bad" kid. But his gnomish aunts and uncles had been quick to foist him off on the temple when his parents hadn't returned from a venture into Farrow. Apparently, there just wasn't enough room—or patience—under the hills for Snoop's curiosity.

As he wandered around, Snoop was startled to find flour on the ground. Miss Pearl *did* get behind on the cleaning sometimes, but not like that. Small footprints ran through it. He knelt closer, tracing one of the prints with his finger. "Cheese, come look at this."

His friend would have been silent as she padded over had she not been loudly licking dairy off her claws. "What?"

He pointed. She crouched next to him, her head cocked as she inspected it. Cheese's nose twitched as she scented the prints. "Not one of us. Could be another gnome."

"Nah. It's a halfling."

"How do you know?"

He pointed to the wide spread of the toes in one of the print. "Halflings hate shoes. They've got them big toes, you see? Mine are tiny."

"Yours are tiny because you're a kid."

He glowered at Cheese, but her green eyes were sparkling with amusement. Shrugging his indignation, he focused on the curious prints. "Who do you think they belong to?"

Cheese shrugged. "A halfling, obviously." He stared her down. Her whiskers twitched in amusement. "Does it matter? Probably someone new at the temple."

With the exception of Anah and Hailee, this didn't seem likely. Miss Pearl was meticulous in her wards. The temple proper was open to any who wandered in, but the back ward which housed the creche was kept strictly off limits.

The wards were good, too. They kept the kids in and the strangers out. Snoop had made numerous attempts at breaking them, only to be put in time-out by Miss Pearl. Then again, she didn't know about the other ways of getting around. The ones that didn't have doors. But it had taken him over a year to discover that. No way some noob halfling would figure it out.

"Nah." Leaning closer, he pointed to where the floured feet had moved away from the spill... and under the table.

He and Cheese bent down, but the space was empty.

"Where'd they go?" Cheese handed Snoop a nearly empty container. She crawled under, her feline nose close to the ground. Soft, sniffing sounds came out until Cheese popped back up on the other side of the table. She was smiling.

"They went in *there*." She pointed up to a vent near the cooking stove. The vent helped move the steam and smoke from cooking out of the temple.

Snoop was simultaneously impressed and anxious. Someone had gotten past Miss Pearl's wards *and* hidden away in the walls. But that meant there was someone in the temple that didn't want to get caught. Worse, if they *had* discovered

Snoop's secret routes, his means of moving around in secrecy might be exposed.

"Should we go in after them?" Cheese made to climb the walls but Snoop shook his head.

"No. We don't know what they got with them. Could have a knife or something."

His friend pointed to a butcher block across the room, the gleam of a knife blade shining like a beacon. "You could take one, too. Make it even. And I have these." She flexed her paw so each claw poked out in warning.

"Nah. I'm just as likely to stick myself and you're about to start clearing the room. Too risky."

As if to punctuate his point, a small, squeaky fart slipped out, and Cheese looked crestfallen. She knew it was only the beginning. Stealth was out. "What should we do then? Tell the teachers?"

It was a sensible proposition. One that Snoop would have considered more if he a) trusted authority and b) didn't know what to do. But he *didn't* trust any authority that wasn't Miss Pearl. Especially not the two new bozos. For all he knew, they were connected to the sneaking halfling. He also knew what to do. Oh, how he knew.

"Nah. We're gonna set some traps. Catch 'em ourselves."

Cheese cackled and Snoop grinned wildly. His stomach grumbled, and he remembered why they'd snuck into the kitchen to begin with. Breakfast had been an atrocious porridge and he'd refused to eat. Now his belly was demanding sustenance.

He climbed up onto the table, looking once more up to the vent. Who was up there? Why?

Whoever it was, they were in for a big surprise.

Something dull and red was tucked under a discarded apron. Snoop crawled over to it and pulled back the apron. On the table was a stupid red rock tied to a stick. It had clearly been misplaced. He picked it up. "What's this?"

"Dunno." Cheese was licking her paw and using it to clean her whiskers. "We should get back before they come to make lunch."

Right. Strange object in hand, Snoop crawled across the table to the cookstove.

On the front part, a low fire kept a murky brown stew of sorts bubbly. "Blech". It was good they'd come on this mission—he could fill up on a snack and avoid the stew.

Behind it was a much larger pot. He used a nearby cloth holder to carefully lift the lid. A heavenly sweet smell wafted out. There was vanilla and the undercurrent of milk and sugar and rice. *Pudding.* His absolute favorite.

Unfortunately, it wasn't done cooking yet. In fact, it only took another glance to discover it was at risk of curdling. The rice hadn't broken down yet but the milk was beginning to skim over.

"Hand me a spoon," he demanded.

"They're all in the dirty dish sink. I'm not washing up anything." Cheese despised water almost as much as she adored dairy.

Snoop contemplated as he stared at the bubbles fighting to pop through the skin on the pudding. Then he looked at the weird stick-rock combo thing in his hand. It had a spoon-like quality and it didn't look dirty...

He stuck it in and stirred.

Snoop was about to try to lick the tip for a taste when Cheese rushed over, ears twitching. "Someone's coming!" she hissed low in the direction of the door.

Ugh. Of all the inconveniences. He dropped the stick thing on the table and scooted off. If he got caught sneaking snacks, Miss Pearl would make sure his meals were extra healthy for weeks. Blech.

Snoop and Cheese had managed to clear most of the room when the door opened. It was the tall one—Hailee. The instinct to run hit Snoop hard, but one look at the woman and he knew he'd never make it. She was the most muscle-bound woman he'd ever seen, and he doubted it was just for show.

"You head back with no fuss," she said, arms crossed, "and I won't say where I found you. Deal?"

Snoop Dug couldn't decide if Hailee was dumber or smarter than she appeared, but he wasn't going to look a gift horse in the mouth. "We just got lost looking for the restrooms."

At that moment, Cheese let a massive fart rip.

Hailee's nose wrinkled. "Somehow, kid, I think you know exactly where the facilities are."

# Chapter Six

W*obble.*

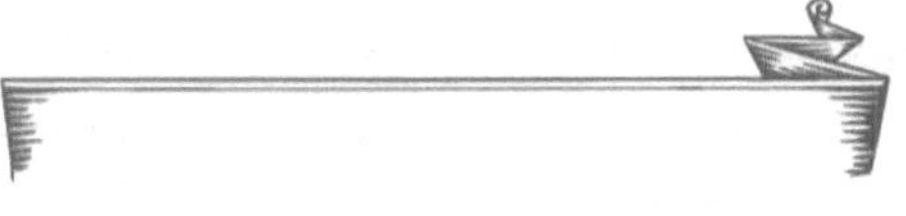

# Chapter Seven

Pearl arrived minutes after Hailee returned with the two escapees. Anah thought her nervous system might collapse. How had she missed *two* absent children? It wasn't as if they had an army of kids.

More like a gaggle, she decided. A gaggle of children. An amount that shouldn't be difficult to supervise.

Though... not once in Anah's life had she been interested in being in charge of a gaggle of children. Or even a single child. She'd lived her adult life with a strict no-child focus.

"HUNGRY!" the twins yelled before plopping themselves down at a table. Anah couldn't get over the juxtaposition of bodies made for brawling and personalities more like gentle butterflies. It was almost... cute.

The acolyte had returned just after Hailee had brought the runaways back in. Their incompetence had narrowly avoided discovery. "Everyone sit, please," Pearl commanded, pitching her voice low and even yet somehow commanding the entire room. How did she do that?

Anah found herself the object of Pearl's scrutiny. After a moment, everyone's eyes were on her. Heat pricked at her cheeks. She'd spent all her life trying to get people's attention, but this was not what she'd had in mind.

"Yes?" she finally said, unsure of what was expected of her.

"It's lunch time," Hailee supplied. This earned her a bright smile from Pearl, which in turn made Hailee's face go scarlet.

"Ah, right. Food." Anah's stomach growled. They hadn't packed anything that morning because, in her naive optimism, she'd assumed they'd have found Bucket by this point.

"Anah, why don't you stay with the children while Hailee helps me get the plates ready."

Pearl was quickly moving up Anah's "vendetta" list. Hailee, of course, looked positively smitten. It was almost enough for Anah to extend some leniency in her dislike. The big goof was chasing after an *acolyte*. Were temple workers even allowed to have relationships?

Anah decided to let Hailee figure it out herself. Relationships were messy enough without a third party offering opinions.

The two disappeared into the kitchen, and Anah was forced to face the gaggle alone.

"Soooo... " she clasped her hands in front of her.

There was a loud gurgle followed by an intense, rotten stench.

"What was *that*?" Anah stared in horror at the children. First flaming sneezes and now this?

"Oh, Cheese, you didn't!" Hope looked close to tears.

Cheese's fur-lined cheeks couldn't visibly blush, but the cat-girl looked properly chagrined. "It was so delicious, though! It's not my fault."

Anah rubbed her temples and attempted to breathe through her mouth. How was this day still *going*? And when would she be able to get back to the task at hand? Bucket and the wand.

"Why don't you sit wherever you sit for lunch," she managed.

The kids scurried to tables and sat in surprising but blessed silence. The door swung wide and Hailee came in bearing a large, heavily burdened tray in each hand, her biceps bulging. Pearl followed and together they walked around the tables, pausing so Pearl could set a plate in front of each child.

Two things occurred to Anah. One was something approaching admiration. Pearl had done this on her own for who knew how long. How many teachers had she trained, only to find herself back in the rough as soon as they'd had enough?

The second understanding was the uncomfortable realization that Anah was just standing there while Pearl and Hailee did all the work. Completely useless. She shouldn't care—this wasn't her actual job, after all. It was a farce. What did it matter if she didn't help out?

But despite her reasoning, Anah found it mattered more than it should. Too embarrassed to ask for direction, she looked around the room, hoping for a clue. It came in the form of stacked pewter cups and a large clay pitcher.

Unsure, she crossed to the items and sniffed at the pitcher. It smelled like water, which was to say, not much at all.

It took most of her strength to lift and tip the massive earthenware pitcher, but Anah managed to fill cups for the children, plus three for the adults. Then, just as cautiously, she handed them out.

"Thanks," Hope said, grasping the cup in small hands and taking a slurp.

"Erm... you're welcome."

When she finished, Anah found Hailee and Pearl looking at her strangely.

"What? If you show me where utensils are, I can hand them out as well. I'm not totally inept."

Anah regretted the words instantly when Hailee smiled deviously. "Does that mean you're *somewhat* inept?"

The children giggled, and Anah's cheeks burned. But Pearl kindly pointed to a small basket near the pitcher. Anah found simple pewter flatware—minus knives—and handed them out as well.

No one was eating.

"Do we..." Anah strained to think. "Say a prayer or something?" After all, it was a temple, and she knew they were big on things like that.

"Oh goodness, no. Dinna is never constant, but always in motion. Growth and change, never stagnant. A habit like praying before meals hinders forward momentum." Pearl's eyes narrowed. "The children are waiting for permission to begin. Which," Pearl's demeanor shifted into something dark and serious, "they will get after I make it clear that there will be no pudding after lunch today."

She began to walk slowly around the tables in a stalking move that reminded Anah of a large and dangerous predator. The twins dared to groan and Hope squeaked, "Unfair!"

"It's quite fair, Hope. Someone has been thieving in the kitchen, and decided to fill their bellies before lunch." Pearl scanned each and every face—even Anah and Hailee's—as if she could discern the culprit just by looking at them.

In a way, it worked. All the children glared at Snoop Dug and Cheese. Snoop promptly protested, hands up. "It weren't us! I stirred it, is all! Didn't even get a lick."

Hope crossed tiny arms over her chest and replied grumpily, "Cheese's bottom says different."

"Nah," said Cheese, licking a paw without a care in the world, "I ate yogurt and some cheddar I found in the fridge. Didn't touch the pudding. Besides, we don't even know if it was a dairy pudding, do we, Miss?"

Anah covered her mouth with her hand at Pearl's triumphant visage. She'd discovered the culprits with hardly any work. *Maybe I should tell her our dilemma. She could flush out Bucket in no time.*

Except Pearl wouldn't have motivation to help, not when it meant losing two more assistants so quickly.

"Well, that does change things. Go on and eat, children."

Anah's anticipation fell flat. That was it? Were there no consequences for these children?

In her day, they'd have been put in their rooms for the rest of the day, no food and no toys. Anah had spent many days alone and hungry, even if something wasn't her fault.

She didn't pout too long—Pearl brought her a plate with stewed meat and greens. Steam wafted off it and she happily dug in. The stew was decent, if a bit bland. Longingly, she thought of the stall in the market and how a few peppers and spices from there would brighten the dish substantially.

As if reading her thoughts, Pearl whispered, "The kids don't much like seasoning, I'm afraid."

That was baffling. "What seasonings have they tried?" There were hundreds of spices. Not all had a kick, even. There was parsley, basil, oregano, and Anah's personal favorite: a blend of dried ground leaves with other spices called *curry*. Surely a few of them would be palatable.

"Well, none." Pearl leaned back, a quizzical look on her face. "I think it's just, well, known here. The novice who trained me explained that children would turn away intense flavors."

Mouth full, Anah spoke through half-chewed food. "You won't know if you don't try."

"Hm."

Despite the flat taste, Anah cleaned her plate. While her magic was still greatly diminished, having a full belly went a long way in helping her not feel completely miserable.

When she and Hailee looked around, she noticed the children's plates were still quite full, with the exception of the twins'. They were each dragging fingers through the remaining sauce on their plate, then licking the digits clean.

*Children are disgusting.*

Pearl cleared her throat. "If you're finished, you may raise your hand, and Anah or Hailee will gather your plates."

All the hands shot up, except the twins again, who were doing their best to clean the plate to shining with their tongues.

There was a lot of remaining food on the plates. With horror, Anah asked Pearl in a low voice, "Does it all go to waste?"

The acolyte offered a sweet smile. "No. We reheat it and let those not as fortunate as us finish it."

Feeling less guilty, Anah and Hailee made quick work of clearing all the dishes.

Anah remembered that rest time was next. Thank the gods. She needed the time to think and regroup.

Pearl clapped her hands once to get everyone's attention. "Now, we shall get our cots—"

"Miss Pearl?" Hope had her hand up.

"Yes?"

"Where's the pudding?"

Pearl schooled her face into a level of sternness that intimidated even Anah. Hailee's eyebrows were raised. "Did you eat your meat? Your vegetables?"

Anah knew for a fact that most of the children had not. A few spoonsful at best, with the rest pushed around to disguise that the portion was mostly unchanged. She wondered if adding flavor would entice the kids to eat more. They were growing and needed food.

Which was something she shouldn't bother thinking about. It wasn't like she'd be there long.

"Well, no, but—"

"How can you have your pudding if you don't eat your meat?" Pearl asked it in such a way that it was clear a response wasn't required. The answer was inherently known by all. No proper food meant no sweets.

The children's crestfallen faces were enough to melt hearts. Pearl's demeanor softened. "I do wish you'd eat your food. As for the pudding, it's all gone. You can thank Snoop Dug and Cheese for that."

The two appeared stricken. Snoop piped up. "We didn't!"

But Pearl was resolute. "Whatever the case, it was in the pot and now it isn't. We can't snack on what isn't there. So please, get your cots and find your places."

A general rumble of complaints and groans filled the classroom. The poor tiny gnome and cat-girl received some violent and accusatory stares. But they had snuck into the kitchen, hadn't they?

"I'm going to take Anah and Hailee into my office for a chat. That does not give you permission to be loud or to play."

More grumbling, but Anah was impressed by how quickly each child had moved their cots to various parts of the room, collecting small toys or slates with chalk to keep them occupied. Pearl was not someone to test boundaries with.

Anah would need to be careful.

She and Hailee followed Pearl out the doo all the way back out to the temple proper.

"I thought we were headed to your office," Hailee said as the three of them stood near the large statue of Dinna.

Pearl gestured to the entirety of the temple. "This is fine. We're a modest place. We've space for pilgrims and patrons, and of course the area with the children. There are places for workers and acolytes to sleep, the creche and the garden, and that's it."

Anah felt couldn't help but feel the attention of the folks gathered in the temple sliding over to her. It occurred to her that, other than a single observation about her horns, the children hadn't cared about her appearance. She'd gone most of the morning with a splitting headache and irritation coming out her ears, but not one bit of judgment.

"How long will they stay quiet?" she asked Pearl, nodding to the warded door.

"I'm sure it's chaos in there now." The acolyte frowned and rubbed at her elbow. She wasn't bothered by the unwatched classroom, yet clearly concerned about something. "Here is where I let you know I've spent the morning watching you."

Both Anah and Hailee stiffened. "How?" Hailee asked, truly puzzled.

"Magic, of course. We're trained in all sorts of magic here, depending on how we can best serve Dinna. In my case, I'm able to scry."

Anah frowned, her head feeling like it was full of tinker parts being shaken around. That would have been useful information to have before. "Why?"

Pearl scoffed. "Obviously, I have the wards on the door, but you can't expect me to let two strangers in with the children with a short interview, no references, and just wash my hands of it? I'm overworked, yes, but not an idiot."

It had seemed incredibly unprofessional and irresponsible of Pearl to just throw the two women to the wolves that were the children. She hated the idea of being watched and raced through her memory to see if anything she'd done jumped out as particularly awful. There was the short-term losing of Snoop and Cheese, but they'd figured it out quickly. That had to count for something, right?

If she weren't so depleted, she'd probably have sensed the magic. But more to the point, Pearl had brought them back out to the temple... which could only mean she was about to kick them out.

It hadn't gone well, sure. But it hadn't gone *that* poorly, had it?

Pearl's face shadowed and she crossed her arms. Anah found herself on the receiving end of the disapproval that seemed to keep the children in line. She understood their obedience much more intimately now. Pearl was absolutely terrifying.

"Neither of you came here for the position, did you?" Her icy gaze slid over to a quite sheepish Hailee. Anah didn't feel any relief. They were busted.

# Chapter Eight

To lie or not to lie, that was the question. The trouble was, neither Anah nor Hailee were particularly strong in the charisma department and their methods of persuasion tended to rely more on violence than honey-coated words.

"Not exactly." Anah spoke slowly, her mind racing. "We came into the temple seeking... something. And then we crossed your path, and—"

To her immense relief, Pearl's face relaxed. She pressed her hands together in front of her heart, her eyes closing. "Dinna works in mysterious ways."

An argument about how preposterous that was sat on the tip of Anah's tongue, but truly, she was too tired and baffled to spit it out. The day had been an absolute absurdity from the minute they'd crossed the temple's threshold and it wasn't even fully over.

"What were your previous occupations?" Pearl was no longer vibrating with accusation.

"Mercenaries, adventurers, and occasional assassins," Hailee listed off proudly. "Though that last one, I'm not sure if it counts, since we only knocked off real assholes."

Pearl arched one eyebrow. "Indeed. And now you're interested in childcare?"

Not in the least. But Pearl was already extending them quite a bit of grace and Anah was certain the honest answer would push it too far. She needed to take control of the conversation.

"We woke up and realized something was missing. It took a bit of time, but our journey led us here. There's something in this temple that we need, I think, and I'd be grateful for the chance to stay long enough to find it." She was becoming quite adept at speaking truths while not being honest in the least. It didn't make Anah feel as good as she would have expected it to.

If Pearl had scrying magic, Anah wasn't sure what other skills she might have. On the one hand, she doubted Pearl's perception. After all, the woman had let them in with scarcely an introduction and entrusted them with the care of children.

On the other hand, there was an edge to Pearl that kept Anah wary. Beyond the scrying, it often felt as if Pearl might be able to look right into Anah's soul.

Who knew what she'd find there?

Therefore, Anah would keep quiet about their real goals as long as possible.

"Ah." Pearl tilted her head, considering. "Well, your leadership over the kids leaves much to be desired. I'll have to fudge that a bit with the parents for now. However, your... martial pasts might make you uniquely perfect for the job. Would you consider staying on the week, at least? Time enough to see if what's missing for you pops into place?"

The idea of being with the children for another five days was appalling, but Anah couldn't help but marvel at how Pearl was able to rebound and flow with every new development.

"That sounds fair. Hailee?" Anah was fairly sure Hailee would agree to jumping off a cliff if it meant spending more time with Pearl.

"Yeah! I mean, cool." Hailee danced a bit on her toes, her delight leaking out.

"Well, that's settled. I'll still be checking in periodically, but this has a ring of destiny to it, doesn't it? I feel you're meant to be here."

Anah wanted to laugh. Pearl's head would spin with how fast they were out of the temple as soon as they found their traitorous halfling and the precious wand he'd stolen.

"You should get back to the children. They're a bit older, so you'll find you can rarely keep them quiet for more than an hour. Hope is the only one who consistently sleeps."

Bewildered, Hailee said, "They seem too old for any sort of nap or quiet time."

Pearl nodded. "They absolutely are. It isn't for them. It's for me, or whoever is watching them. They are sweet, but gods, they can wear me out!"

Wasn't that the truth? Anah startled herself by chuckling. With the other women staring at her in surprise, she felt pressured to add, "They sure do!"

With that, Pearl escorted them back to the classroom. Once more, they bypassed the wards with no issues, through the kitchen and straight to the classroom door. Anah ignored the feeling building within that she was not the one doing the tricking, but the one being tricked. There were some hushed murmurs coming through, but not the chaos Anah expected.

All the children were still on their cots when she stepped in the room. It was blissfully quiet and the pounding in her head lessened.

She and Hailee pulled chairs close together, with Hailee's knees uncomfortably high in the too-small chair.

"I can't believe she's letting us stay," Anah whispered.

"I mean, other than losing the kids to the kitchen, we haven't had much time to screw up." Hailee had a contemplative look on her face. It was not a look Anah was used to seeing.

"What? You're sad the kids ate all the pudding?"

"I don't think they did eat it." Hailee's mouth turned down. "It was still bubbling when I walked out with them. I'm thinking Bucket's sneaking into the kitchen and eating their food."

Anah could slap herself. Of course. If she wasn't so worn out, she was certain the connection would have occurred to her first.

"Clever, Hailee." Her friend beamed at the compliment. Anah didn't hand them out often, though that might be due to growing up without hearing them much, either. She glanced around to make sure the kids weren't listening. So far, it seemed none of them paid much notice to the grown women at all.

"Pearl sure is pretty," Hailee said it with a sigh, like a soft afterthought. "I'm glad we get a week here."

Anah straightened. "We're not here for fun. We have a halfling to discover. Don't lose sight."

Her friend drooped. "Yeah, I know. It's just, I know you're probably pretty tired."

"What does that have to do with chatting up pretty acolytes?" Anah knew she sounded sharp, but having her weakness pointed out was a trigger.

If her tone stung, Hailee didn't show it. "Because you can take it easy while we look. I'm getting some ideas about how to use the kids to our benefit. Also, Pearl said she's been scrying, right? If she likes me, maybe I can... I don't know... get her to look for Bucket."

For a moment, Anah worried that she and Hailee had traded places. That she was suddenly the oafish sidekick and her friend the brilliant mastermind. Only, she knew, she truly was exhausted and Hailee had never been *stupid* so much as infuriatingly laid-back.

It was easy to misinterpret Hailee's ability to be happy almost anywhere with dullness, but it boiled down to her genuinely not needing much in life.

*What must that be like?*

"Truly good thinking," Anah said grudgingly. "If we asked her now, she'd be perturbed at the ruse. But if we help her for the week—"

"She might help us."

"Shit." Anah pinched the bridge of her nose so her hand blocked the smile fighting to the surface. "This blunder has turned into a good plan."

"I have those sometimes," Hailee said, rolling her shoulders.

Maybe she did, and Anah hadn't been good at listening. Something she'd think about more when she didn't have so much on her plate.

# Chapter Nine

"I swear it on Under the Hill," Snoop said solemnly. "We didn't eat the pudding. But we know who did."

The others were on their cots, leaning in close to hear his whispering.

"Who?" Stump asked. Stump and Bruiser loved pudding dearly and were still nursing hurt feelings. "You think it was the new teachers?"

Snoop wrinkled his nose. "No, dummy! The one with the horns was in here with you the whole time, and the one who looks like she could fight a bear and win was only in the kitchen for a second. But me and Cheese found something."

"You found dairy," Hope accused. Still holding a grudge, then. "Which is just rude. We're the ones who suffer."

Cheese had, at least, chosen the far corner of a room to place her cot. It only helped the smallest amount. Guilt tiptoed into Snoop's belly, making itself warm and solid in there. The goal had been to fetch snacks, but he'd been so distracted he hadn't stopped Cheese.

It was his job to watch out for the others. He knew better than them how little adults could be trusted to keep their best interests at heart. Like his parents, who'd come to Farrow to try and set up a trading hub for Underhill, only to be swindled out of all their savings.

His aunts and uncles had dropped him off at the temple, swearing they'd return when they'd saved enough to pay off the debt collectors.

Which was, he assumed, never, as it was difficult for gnomes to make much of a living. Too small for many commercial trades, too strange-looking for customer service, too kind-hearted to be savvy.

Well, he was going to change that. He was going to prove to the gnomes—and to the people of Farrow—that while small in stature, a hob could have big ideas. Large inventions. And reap huge amounts of respect. He'd be king of the Underhill.

"I'm sorry about that, Hope, really I am."

"I'm not." Cheese stretched and curled up on her cot, knees tucked under her chin and tail curled around her. The girl was flexible, great at fitting into odd spaces and sneaking about. If she could manage her diet, Snoop was certain Cheese could be an amazing thief or assassin. Something very neat, at least.

If she'd stop letting her body give her away.

"Shut up, Cheese, you're not helping. Anyways, like I was saying, me and Cheese figured out someone's been sneaking about in the temple. We saw their footprints and everything."

That had everyone's attention. Snoop reveled in it. He liked being the leader. The twins were two years younger than his nine and already bigger than him. Soon, they'd tower over the rest of them and, while their hearts were delicate as roses, their strength was formidable. Cheese was also taller, but she walked low enough he rarely felt small compared to her.

Hope was practically a baby at six years old, and Stevie was... well, Stevie. They'd stay the same for another decade, then shoot up in growth, decide their gender—if they wanted to—and begin to speak all in one go.

"Why would someone be sneaking through the temple?" Hope asked. "If they just asked Miss Pearl, I bet she'd give them whatever they needed."

"If they're sneaking through, they must be up to no good." Snoop felt certain on this point. No one would crawl through the vents of the temple, which allowed the air to move around. They were hot and stuffy and chiseled out of the stone. In some places, the stone had crumbled and collapsed, blocking the way.

He'd spent a year exploring them and all he'd discovered was that there were many less miserable ways to sneak around.

Just to make sure they were on his side, though, he added, "I bet it was them that ate our pudding."

"That's messed up," Stomp said sadly.

"Exactly. Who knows what else they'll do if no one catches them?" The gears in his mind were already cranking, his pulse racing to meet them. So many *ideas*.

Hope slid her finger into a nostril. "Should we tell Miss Pearl?"

"Nah. You know she's got those two hacks in here because she's bloody tired, right?" He gazed solemnly at all of them. "She's overworked and underappreciated by the grownups. She's been taking extra good care of us, but she needs a rest. Now it's time for us to take care of her—by catching the sneak in the temple."

All the other's faces lit up in understanding and resolve, and Snoop relaxed, knowing he had them. And wouldn't Miss

Pearl be so impressed with them when they bagged the pudding thief? She'd see they were more mature than she thought, and she could get rid of the new teachers.

"So, we're agreed, right?"

Everyone nodded. Snoop beamed. "Good. Then we tell the teachers our chores are in the garden today."

"I hate the garden," Hope said, pulling her finger out and looking to see if she'd gotten anything good. "It's hot."

"And if Stevie's not careful, they'll set the food on fire," Cheese pointed out.

Snoop shrugged. "It's just the veg that'll burn up. Then we don't have to eat it."

"Stevie's coming for sure, then." Cheese tucked her head back in, having contributed to the plan.

As he thought this over, a plan formed more fully in his mind. "That's perfect, really," Snoop said as the tracks of his plan began to lay in order. "Stevie, you mind setting stuff on fire?"

The dragonling's eyes twinkled as they shook their head. They didn't mind at all.

That was all the distraction Snoop would need to get into the shed where the fertilizer and other supplies were.

"Okay." He started to lay back on his cot.

"I have a question," Hope said.

Snoop bit back a curse. She was young and a human and it wasn't right to hold those things against her, even if they made her extra annoying.

There was a jiggle of the knob at the door. "Hurry up, teachers are back."

"Have you ever played 'Duck, Duck, Go Screw Yourself?' Miss Anah said we could play it but I don't know the rules."

The door swung open just in time to save Snoop from having to answer.

# Chapter Ten

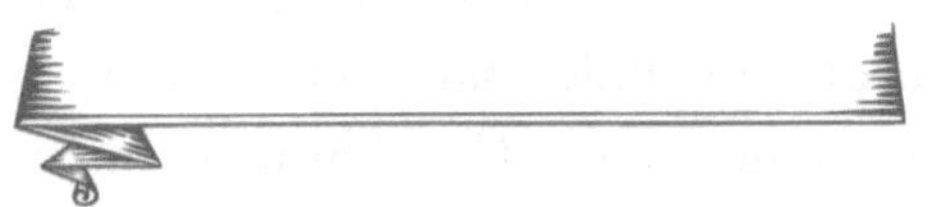

Certain she was going to regret it, Anah asked the kids, "How do you go about chores?"

Based on their immediate and borderline diabolical reaction, she knew she'd stepped in it.

"Today is working in the garden," Cheese answered. "Helping to weed and water and stuff. "S'posed to help us learn about the ecosystem."

It sounded dubious at best, but really, what choice did they have? Hailee and she were winging it. To Anah's consternation, Hailee was adapting far quicker than she was to the situation. The only thing that made Anah feel better about it was assuming Hailee's innate easy-going nature helped her identify with the gaggle of children. Anah couldn't be faulted for being a bit grumpy.

"Then I suppose that's where we'll go."

Hailee chimed in. "Before we do, please put your cots back up, along with any toys you used during quiet time."

To Anah's complete amazement, the children did as they were asked. No complaints or dawdling, with the exception of Hope, who'd been distracted by small wooden figurines. She was setting up some sort of scene with them and didn't notice when her mates had finished and lined up.

"Hope," Hailee said with a stern edge Anah hadn't heard before, "it's time to do chores. The toys will be there for you to play with later."

"They might not be," Hope whined. "The others might come grab them up first. They're bigger than me." There was a small slick of snot under one nostril. Hope wiped it away with the back of her hand. "Can I bring them with me to the garden?"

"No, you may not." Hailee's hands were on her hips. Usually when they were in that area, it was to pull out weapons and tear through mobs of attackers. Somehow, her stance now was just as intimidating. Anah felt a stab of jealousy, then, a feeling she rarely allowed herself to experience.

*If I was tall and not fell-touched, people would listen to me like they're listening to her. Hailee's just got genetics on her side.*

But the reasoning fell flat, and Anah worked hard to tuck away the envy before it had a chance to fester.

THE TEMPLE'S GARDEN was a surprising delight. Anah found herself in a large courtyard, the middle of which was a veritable bounty of lush, green plants and several fruit trees. It was the kind of place that she would have loved to spend time in as a child... had she been allowed. Memories of the past were bubbling up with increasing frequency and she despised it. Anah was ready to get this job over with. After all, the past was behind you for a reason.

"Ok," she said to the group of children. "What do we do next?"

The kids looked at each other and shared smiles that left Anah distinctly uncomfortable. She was missing something, some inside joke where she was the punchline. But seeing as this was her first foray into childcare, she had to wait and see just how devious they would turn out to be.

Hailee pointed to the well and said, "I bet I need to pull up water, yeah?"

Snoop nodded eagerly. "Yes, we need to water all the plants and do the weeding."

Cheese piped up, "And also pick things if they look yummy!"

Hope scrunched her nose, "Nothing in the garden looks yummy. It's all vegetables."

Once more, Anah had the thought that if the children had been served vegetables roasted or sauteed with spice, rather than boiled and plain, they may not find the dishes so disagreeable. Preparation methods were almost as vital as seasoning when it came to delighting the palate.

"Okay," she agreed. "That sounds like a plan." After that, it was a matter of dividing the children amongst the rows, grabbing a basket for herself, and watching as Hailee began to haul up water from the well with ease, her arms flexing.

Anah lost herself in the fresh scents of tilled earth and cut leaves as she moved through the garden, doing as the children were: weeding, finding ripe tomatoes, eggplants, zucchini, feeling the warmth of the sun on her neck and the gentle ache of stooping over to do hard work. Her head still pounded and her body was still exhausted, but there was something refreshing about sunlight and not having to worry about death or misadventure striking from any corner. Also, she didn't need to constantly speak with her wards.

They went on like this for a while, and Anah noticed how dry the garden had gotten. She wondered if Pearl had been unable to tend to the children and work the well. Some of the leaves crumbled all too easily between her fingers, and it was a wonder that the garden still managed to produce as it did. Perhaps that was some of the influence of Dinna, taking her role in growth literally when it came to feeding her patrons.

As they worked, she fell into the tunnel vision of hyper-fixating on a project. Anah was attuned to the job, with everything else—including the children—disappearing from her focus. And of course, that was Anah's mistake. That was immediately apparent when she heard Stevie begin to sniffle somewhere across the garden. Standing up with a jerk, she whipped around to see where the dragonling was. It was too far. She'd never make it in time. Neither would Hailee, who was looking panicked next to the well.

Stevie gave an enormous "Ah, Ah *Ahhhh*!" and sneezed. "*Chooooooooooo*". Fire blossomed from his nostrils, scorching the plants in his direct vicinity. The poor garden vegetables were so thirsty, so dried out, that they caught like kindling. The fire burst up, and Stevie's arms pinwheeled as he rocked back and scrambled away from the flames.

Anah stared at the rapidly moving fire, knowing that if it were to consume the garden, not only would she and Hailee lose the ability to search for Bucket from within temple walls, but also (and there was a niggling guilt she did not enjoy when she considered this) that they would be taking food literally from the mouths of babes. That was a level of low that even

Anah, with all her selfish ambition, was not interested in stooping to. She and Hailee met gazes across the garden and nodded. It was one of the many benefits of working so closely with someone for so long. There had been a time recently, when she, Bucket, and Hailee had all been able to act without speaking, working as one to tackle whatever obstacle confronted them. But Bucket was gone, and Anah couldn't linger on the feelings that accompanied his absence. Instead, she used what she had on hand—her fell blood.

Fire was minimally taxing for her. It came naturally because it stirred in her very blood. It was why Anah had to work constantly to control her temper, and why she tried to stay away from flammable things when control was no longer possible. In this particular case, though, she allowed her feelings of panic and fear to release within, stretching until her skin lit up with its own blue flame, hungry and hot and eager for the same things that Stevie's fire yearned for—oxygen and something to burn.

Not feeling the lick of fiery heat, she walked into the already scorched garden. Her own flames sucked up all the oxygen in the vicinity, starving out Stevie's sneezed blaze. While she was doing this, she heard the children gasp as Hailee launched herself up and into the well, while Anah kept trying to slow the burn. She knew what Hailee was doing. Those monk-strong arms and legs were helping her scurry down to the bottom of the well. In only a matter of moments, mere breaths, Hailee was back up, the fire around Anah already dwindling as it fought for fuel. Soaked from head to toe and dripping, Hailee launched herself at the embers and coals and lingering flames and rolled. Her wet body squashed out the remainder of the fire.

When she was thoroughly coated in a mixture of mud and ash, Hailee stood. She and Anah went around, kicking soil on any last sparks. They'd managed to save more than three quarters of the garden and all the fruit trees. It wasn't great, Anah knew, but it wasn't nothing either. A spark of pride swelled in her chest, and this was added to when she and Hailee spun around and found the children huddled together, staring at them in awe.

Cheese was the first to speak, her jaw slightly open as she said, "How did you know to do that?"

Anah shrugged, and she and Hailee shared a look. Hailee spoke. "One time, we had a job that required us to sneak through the lair of a fire-imp. Unfortunately, at the time, our sneaking skills weren't top-notch and the imp discovered our presence. Trapped in a cave like that, it began to burn everything. And while Anah couldn't be immediately hurt, even she is susceptible to flames eventually. Anah was the one who began to try to fight fire with fire. While Bu—" Hailee stopped herself from saying the name of their missing partner, the one who had betrayed them and led them to standing in the middle of a garden, inside a temple of a deity that had never appealed to Anah in all her years.

"That's when I," Hailee corrected, "realized that if I could douse myself in the water from our canteens, it would slow my risk of burning. And"—and she looked quite pleased with herself as she said this—"you should know that if you stop, drop, and roll, the flames will smother out."

Anah smirked, "Just don't stop, drop, and roll straight into the fire, like Hailee did. That's for dumb grownups who can deal with the consequences of their actions."

Hailee laughed and then winced. There were light, pinking ribbons of burns starting to poke up along her muscular arms and her singed pants. The dampness of the well had at least helped her clothing survive so that the only awkwardness Anah and Hailee had to face was accounting for the fire in the first place, not Hailee's sudden nudity in front of children. There was a huge sense of relief as she stared at what could have been an absolute disaster but with quick thinking had only ended up being a medium inconvenience.

At that moment, Snoop Dug emerged from a small wooden shed, carrying a bucket and several shovels. He stared at the smoke-filled courtyard, his nose wrinkling, ashes still floating in the air, and said, "What the heck happened out here?"

# Chapter Eleven

G*obble... gobble...*
   *Wobble.*

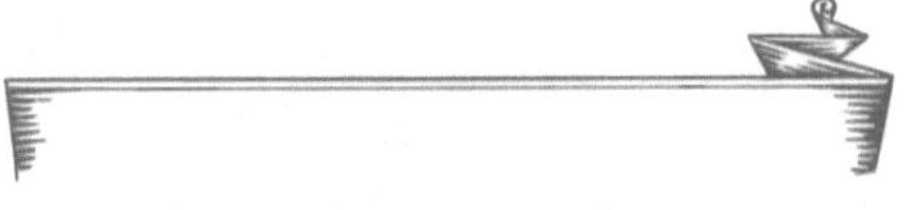

# Chapter Twelve

After making sure all the children were truly unscathed, Anah went to Stevie, who was looking as embarrassed as a dragonling could look. The poor kid. She knew they couldn't speak, couldn't explain or say they were sorry, and it wasn't Stevie's fault that they had a cold and a penchant for flames. Anah wanted to say something to them, but wasn't quite sure what when the door to the courtyard burst open and an irate Pearl came storming out.

The acolyte's eyes went wide as she surveyed the damage to the garden. Then they moved with weapon-like efficiency to spear Hailee and Anah. Damn. Anah had not been on the receiving end of a teacher's accusatory look like that in several decades, yet she discovered it had the same debilitating effect now as it had when she was a young child.

"What," Pearl huffed, her voice tremorous, "happened?"

Hailee managed to shrink in on herself, and Anah was momentarily relieved to discover she wasn't the only person affected by Pearl's rage. The children moved quickly to circle Stevie, creating a protective ring around them. Her stomach soured. It had been an accident, and yet the children were already prepared to shield their playmate. Pearl seemed an all-right woman, though Anah had only known her for the day. The children's reactions scratched at an old wound deep within and forced her to remember what it had been like to be the child blamed for everything. Was Stevie that child in this group?

When Anah was young and her emotions too large for her very small body, accidents like this had been the norm. The orphanage where she'd lived had decided that the best way to handle her fiery temper was to keep her away from the children. And the garden. And the food. And, Anah had to admit, basically everything. It had been a lonely childhood and one in which she had too much time to think of all the reasons why she felt so small—not just literally, but in her heart. It hadn't been until she aged out of the orphanage, met Hailee, and started her own adventuring group, that Anah had managed to grow into herself and decide that it was critical she become a person people respected and listened to, the kind of person who could never be pushed away and could never be alone again.

Drawing her shoulders back, Anah moved in front of Stevie as well. "It was an accident," she said. "Stevie has a cold and they found something outside that made them sneeze."

Pearl's eyebrow arched, but she didn't disagree. "Why then," she asked Anah, "didn't you clear their nostrils before coming outside?"

*Clear their nostrils?* Anah thought. Was that also something she was supposed to do? Based on Pearl's long-suffering reaction, Anah was making a face that explained just how little they understood about the care and keeping of children. It was a bit of a bite to Anah's pride, as she'd been proud of the fact that she and Hailee had managed to tackle the fire before it had done too much damage and successfully kept the children safe at the same time.

Pearl pulled a large square piece of cloth from inside the sleeve of her robe and walked over to Stevie. This might be better: She wrapped a corner around a finger and wiped out the inside of Stevie's nostrils. The crust that had formed there disappeared, and the look of relief at Stevie's next deep breath sent an arrow of guilt into Anah's chest. It was such a simple thing to do and yet neither she nor Hailee had thought of it.

Switching the cloth to another corner, Pearl then wiped the absolute disgusting mess that was Hope's nose. The other children quickly took their sleeves and made sure their own noses were clean before Pearl could come and minister to them.

"There," Pearl said, sounding a little too patronizing, "That's how you do it. I know it can be difficult working with a dragonling, but"—here Pearl stared Anah down—"you of all people should know how to take care when combustibles are near flames."

At this, Pearl looked to the sky, measuring where the sun was; the sundial in the courtyard's shadow made it look to be nearing dinner. "I suppose, that this was a good marker for the end of your first day. Children, go inside and freshen up for your parents, please. I need to have a small chat with Anah and Hailee."

This was the second "small chat" in a day and Anah wasn't looking forward to it.

The children slinked back into the temple, occasionally shooting furtive glances at Anah and Hailee. Anah braced herself for what was surely going to be an awful dressing-down.

But Pearl only sighed, the weight of the day evident on the acolyte's shoulders.

"I'm sorry," Pearl said.

Anah shook herself. She wasn't used to apologies, certainly not after any sort of disaster like the one that had just occurred.

Pearl finger-combed her hair out of its braid and then began to re-braid it. Hailee's eyes locked on the smooth, rhythmic motions of Pearl's fingertips, but Anah remained on edge.

"This has been a difficult school to be in charge of," Pearl admitted. "The parents of these children have high expectations. In a lot of ways, Snoop is the easiest to deal with, despite his penchant for creating more trouble than good, because at least when he does something mischievous, the only people I have to face are the other temple acolytes and priests. When the others get picked up, I'll have to tell the parents that there was a fire."

She looked at them with pleading in her bright blue eyes. "Can you imagine what it's like to explain to a massive orc and his equally strong warrior wife that their twins were trapped in a courtyard with a fire? Or the absolute pissy attitude of an ornwas when he discovers that his eldest daughter had been this close to fire?" Pearl pinched her forefinger and thumb close together.

"Let's not even talk about the hot mess that are Hope's moms when they find out their precious baby could have been hurt. Even Stevie's parents, though understanding of how accidents can occur, expect us to be on watch to prevent things like this from happening."

Hailee leaned back. "But you're just one person," she argued. "How are you supposed to make sure that all these kids are safe all the time?"

Pearl let out a bitter chuckle. "That's exactly the problem, isn't it? Not only am I one person, but I'm one person who is in charge not just of their education but also maintaining the temple of Dinna. Ensuring that they are fed. Ensuring that they are safe. Ensuring that they grow up to be citizens of Farrow in a way that is beneficial and speaks well of them, of me, and of my goddess."

Anah could feel the weight of Pearl's life shifting onto her tiny shoulders. She shook from the pressure of it. And she'd thought that being in an adventuring group was difficult. But she worked with two competent adults who were able to make their own decisions and be responsible for their own safety and participation. It had been one day, Anah understood. Just one day, and already they'd misplaced two children, they'd set the garden on fire, and she'd barely made decent conversation with anyone of any age due to the splitting migraine now taking over her head.

No wonder Pearl was so desperate for aid that she would let two strangers step in and take over. Even if she was watching from her scrying-place, Pearl had to have needed the break, no matter how short or flimsy it was.

"I'm sorry," Anah apologized, surprising herself as well as Pearl. "We should have considered the potential for Stevie's sneezes. I wish that I had been better prepared." And she meant it. Anah liked having a plan. She liked knowing where things were going and how she would deal with them. Being in this school, in this creche, in the middle of Farrow, was an experience that was bewildering and humbling—two emotions Anah hadn't been interested in feeling.

Pearl nodded. "I believe you. And contrary to how it might sound, I do want you here. It's selfish, of course, but also, the children seem to like you. That hasn't always been the case."

That, at least, Anah doubted. She'd done nothing to earn their admiration. If anything, they'd walked all over her and Hailee. If they liked them at all, it was because the adults now in charge of their care were complete and clueless pushovers.

"Why don't you go home and rest?" Pearl said. "And please consider coming back tomorrow."

Hailee was about to agree, but Pearl held up her hand and shook her head. "No, I mean it. I want you to really consider whether you'll be able to do this job another day. Every day you're here is a blessing for us, but it isn't one that should be treated carelessly." She reached into a pocket of those robes that seemed to produce never-ending supplies and pulled out a pouch of silver. She tossed it over, and Hailee caught it from mid-air. "This is for a day's work. Usually we prefer to pay for the week in one go, but I don't want you to leave here feeling cheated should you choose not to return."

Anah was surprised. This sort of generosity and trust wasn't something that she or Hailee came across on the regular. It almost always took haggling to get even a quarter of the promised pay up front, and sometimes it took violence to remind clients to pay at the end of a job. She nodded in thanks.

Despite the failure to find Bucket, Anah was more than grateful to leave the temple. Her body ached and her head pounded.

But worse than that, she couldn't find a way to shut off the new emotions stampeding through her chest.

# Chapter Thirteen

When they finally returned to the Drunken Goat, Anah bypassed the bar, Marcus, and his wife, and stumbled up the stairs to the small room she shared with Hailee. She flopped face down onto the bed. Her entire body was a groan.

It may have been minutes or hours, it didn't really matter, when Hailee slipped into the door, saying, "I brought some food." The rattle of a bowl being set on the table barely made a dent in Anah's fugue.

A moment later, the bed dipped and Anah felt Hailee rubbing a gentle circle on her back. They weren't particularly affectionate friends, but Anah discovered that it was the best thing she hadn't known she needed. It took tremendous effort, but Anah managed to roll over and look up at her friend.

"I don't think I can do that again," she told Hailee.

"Not what you expected?"

"You can say that again," Anah answered. Her eyes were sandy, the grit of exhaustion making every blink a painful trial. "I don't understand how any of us survive into adulthood. How can they be so awful and so taxing yet so tiny?"

Hailee brought the bowl of stew over and Anah spooned it into her mouth, not even tasting it.

After she'd finished, Anah handed the bowl back to Hailee. Her friend moved quietly, and Anah allowed herself to sink further into the mattress, preparing for sleep. Hailee wasn't ready to stop the conversation, though.

"But we are going to return tomorrow, aren't we?"

The pleading tone that carried Hailee's question prompted Anah to look up at her, trying to parse out just what it was her friend was asking. Had they not spent the day in the same school? Had Hailee been dragged into some alternate reality?

The forlorn look on Hailee's face was one Anah had never seen before. "Is this about Pearl?"

"No... maybe... yes?" Hailee scratched at the back of her hair, trying to look less awkward, which somehow made her even more awkward than ever.

Irritation tried to scrabble through Anah's body, but she was simply too tired to feel anything at all. "We will have to go back. So long as Bucket is in that temple, we need to be in that temple as well." Though Anah couldn't imagine at this point what Bucket was doing hiding in a temple of Dinna for so long, or... at all.

Hailee's shoulders sagged with relief. It was curious, this new interest Hailee had. In the past, Anah's friend had been game for whatever quest Anah wanted to take up, for whatever adventure she and Bucket tugged the monk along on. While Hailee had had a string of dalliances across Deladrin, there had never been a time when Hailee's interest had remained piqued for so long (long being more than a few hours). There was something strange and tugging in Anah's chest and she didn't understand nor wish to know what it was.

Instead of pressing Hailee about Pearl, Anah asked "How are you so good with kids?" Because that had been a shock, hadn't it? Watching Hailee's comfort when working with tiny creatures who seemed to Anah to be just as dangerous and potentially evil as many of the monsters they encountered in their travels.

Hailee chuckled softly. "I wasn't always a monk, you know." She moved over to her bed and stretched out, turning to face Anah and propping her head up on her arm. "I grew up on my parents' farm with nine siblings. I was the eldest and helped out with my siblings."

Anah's body seemed to freeze over with fear at the mere idea of having nine siblings. *That was nine too many*, she thought, but kept that thought to herself. "So then what happened?"

"Unfortunately, while they had many hands to help with the farm, there wasn't enough coin so that all of us could eat." A shadow passed over Hailee's face. "When we got older, we got to have a choice. Either we could be married off in the hopes of finding a better family that could provide more, or we could move to a monastery, who sometimes would pay for new recruits. I knew even back then that I had no interest in being married off, so I chose the monastery instead. When I was nine, I went to the temple of Nym, but the thing about monasteries is, you live with even more people crowding around, so that there is a real sense of family."

Hailee's tale continued to sound like an absolute nightmare to Anah. How had they not talked about this during their years of traveling together? Anah had known that Hailee had been a devotee of Nym's, and she had known that Hailee grew up on a farm. But the actual means and reasons for shifting from one place to another and then to joining Anah had never been something that came up. A small worm of guilt niggled at Anah's chest as she understood she'd never asked Hailee about her past. Making Anah, she supposed, quite selfish.

"Why did you decide to leave the monastery to come with me?" Anah sat up just a little bit, the smallest bit that her exhausted body could manage. "At the time you told me that it was so you'd see the world, but we haven't seen that much of the world and you've been content." Something occurred to Anah and she tacked on, "You have been content, right?"

"Oh yeah," Hailee offered her a gentle smile. "Seeing the world was the kind of answer that felt generic enough that anyone would believe it." Anah wanted to laugh, because it was a generic answer and she had believed it. "But the truth of it was, I hadn't had a day of privacy in my entire life." Hailee rolled onto her back and stared at the ceiling "And while traveling with you and Bucket isn't the same as being on my own, I knew that I wasn't prepared for complete isolation. But occasionally I have my own room, or tent, or days off to explore. And the two of you always respect my space and my things."

That was interesting information Anah wanted to absorb and turn over, but unfortunately her brain was about the consistency of the pudding that had gone missing at lunch. "Do you still want that privacy and sense of freedom?"

"I don't know what I want." Hailee let out a soft sigh "I think I enjoyed having someone else make all the decisions for me, but today in the temple, working with those kids, I realized how important it is that I learn to make my own decisions as well."

Anah didn't know how to respond to that. In part because it almost sounded like Hailee was considering leaving the group. If she left the band, then Anah would be all by herself. No Bucket, no Hailee, no jobs as of yet, and that was something she couldn't bear to consider. "Well, just know that we can always change things up a bit," Anah said, hoping she could persuade Hailee to stay. "Just know that I am open to you making decisions for us in the future."

Hailee barked out a startled laugh. "Ha! You don't know how to let other people have control."

It didn't sound like an accusation or as if it were intended to be mean-spirited, but Hailee's words struck Anah like an arrow all the same, sharp and punching straight to the heart. She didn't think she was *that* controlling. She'd assumed that because Bucket and Hailee never mentioned any wants or needs that they saw Anah as a sort of leader for their group. Anah toyed with the thought that perhaps that had been what pushed Bucket away.

There wasn't time to ruminate, though, as Hailee asked, "Why are you so terrible with kids?" And then as an aside, "They're practically the same size as you. I just assumed you would be on an even playing field with them."

If anyone else had made that joke, Anah probably would have set them on fire. As it was, Hailee, who'd made plenty of height jokes through the duration of their working together (and she was so tired she wasn't sure she actually could), Anah let it slide. "I don't know why I'm so terrible with kids... and maybe also with people." When Hailee chuckled at that, Anah cracked a smile. "Yeah, laugh it up, buster. I'm aware that I rub people the wrong way. When you grow up half-fell and with horns like mine, people tend to not give you the benefit of the doubt."

"You think people don't respond well to you because of who you are?"

Anah could feel Hailee's eyes on her, even as the room darkened, night coming fast outside. The single candle was the only remaining light.

"It's not that, Anah." Hailee offered. "It's that you're kind of an asshole. Or, at the very least, bossy and blunt."

"I prefer to think of myself as having leadership capabilities." Anah replied tartly. "But yes, I know for a fact that my heritage plays a part in how the world treats me."

When Hailee didn't reply and the single candle began to flutter and gutter out, Anah found she had more to say. Maybe the darkness was a protective blanket, shielding her from the consequences of admitting anything out loud. But in that moment, she felt safe enough to offer a bit of herself to Hailee. "I grew up in a temple like Dinna's."

Anah moved just enough to pull the scratchy wool blanket over her body. She didn't care that she hadn't washed, or brushed her teeth, or waxed her horns. Sleep was just on the edge of her horizon. And as soon as she was done telling Hailee about herself, she planned on passing out and pretending like it had never happened.

"Well, not exactly like Dinna's temple. Like Snoop, I lived there after my mother left me at their doorstep. She was human and didn't know how to raise a fell child. Nor did she want to leave me with my father, to be raised in the demon realm."

Anah snuggled in deeper, letting the warmth of the wool pull her down, closer to sleep. "But while I was a ward of the temple, the novices who ran it also didn't know much about fell-touched. And what they did know did not leave much confidence. And so I was left alone a lot of the time, and ostracized by the other children when I wasn't by myself."

Anah swallowed past the lump forming in her throat. She knew how sad her story sounded when she said it out loud. She hated how very "Waaah, I'm so sad about me" it came across, and it marked her with a weakness that could easily be exploited in the wrong hands.

Hailee's voice drifted across through the darkness. "I didn't know that. You always sounded so confident when you talked about your life and school, that I assumed it was a happy place for you."

Anah shrugged before realizing that Hailee wouldn't see it in the low light of the room. "It's easier to be respected if people don't feel pity for you."

Anah willed the light of the candle to finally sputter out, leaving them in complete darkness. She didn't know how she would handle another day, but there wasn't really a choice now was there. A myriad of fears crossed through her mind in the dark, warring with each other. What if they didn't find Bucket? What if Hailee decided to leave her? What if all of this left Anah alone with only a handful of silver coins and a great distaste for temples and children?

Before she could slip into anxiety-filled dreams, though, Hailee whispered into that inky blackness "I don't know. I think the kids don't pity you, and they certainly seemed to like you despite your heritage."

# Chapter Fourteen

When the morning light filtered through the thick and dusty glass of their room, Anah woke with more energy than she'd had the day before. Which wasn't saying much, as yesterday she'd been real freaking tapped. But she at least had enough energy that she could get up, stretch, dress herself, and look over to Hailee.

Something had changed between them in the quiet of the night before, and Anah mused on the fact that they had spent so much time together, years fighting, traveling, joking, et cetera, but had never actually gotten to know each other. What was it that made her so reluctant to ask Hailee about her past?

Actually, Anah knew the answer. Because if she'd asked Hailee to talk about herself, then her friend would have expected the same in return. Anah had worked hard to leave the temple and her loneliness and the abandonment of her childhood behind. That wasn't who she was. It wasn't who she was going to be. She'd already experienced life as a small, lonely person who was rarely listened to and often blamed. Now that she was an adult, she was working her butt off so that didn't happen again.

How she was going to do that, though, relied heavily on the Wand of Birramos.

Hailee and she stumbled down and ate breakfast, barely speaking to each other or the innkeepers. It was as if Hailee understood that Anah needed time to recover from exposing even the smallest bit of herself that she had, and for that Anah was grateful.

"So, uh, we're going back to the school?" Hailee asked, her mouth half-full of porridge drizzled with honey and splashed with cream.

Anah nodded, "Bucket's still trapped." She stirred her spoon in her bowl thoughtfully, watching the dried fruit mix in with the oats. "Besides, as obnoxious as our cover story is, it allows us access to the temple we'd never have otherwise."

"No magic?" asked Hailee, a surprised look on her face. "But you're always so good at spell work."

Something akin to pride flared inside Anah's tiny chest. She wasn't used to the feeling, but discovered that she rather liked it. "I am good at those things, aren't I?" She stirred again and lifted a bite to her mouth. After chewing, she added, "But I'm afraid I have nothing left of Bucket's to make finding him easier. Tracing someone without an item of theirs is quite difficult, and until I can get some fell water, I'm running very close to empty."

Hailee shrugged. "Cool."

Anah rolled her eyes and stifled a laugh. Her body ached from the antics of the day before, but she found herself moving with, maybe not a pep in her step, but something light as they made their way through the market and to the temple of Dinna. As they walked, Hailee brought up the very thing Anah had been considering that morning. "Why do you think we never talked before? You know, really talked."

Anah didn't miss a step. "Probably because I assumed I'd never stick around with any one person for very long." That wasn't the entire truth, but Anah wasn't ready to admit how afraid she was of loneliness. And more than that, how convinced she was that loneliness was her destiny. "You're the one stupid enough to stick around with me. That's on you."

This earned her a laugh, and Hailee slapped her, perhaps a little too hard, on the back of her shoulder. "I did stick around, didn't I?" Hailee moved in closer, so that their strides almost matched. Almost but not quite, as Hailee's legs were so long and it took one-and-a-half steps for Anah to make up for every one of her friend's. " You shouldn't be so hard on yourself. You're pretty easy to travel with, you know."

Anah turned her head to look at her friend, eyebrow raised. "Am I?"

"Yeah." Hailee met her gaze, if only for a moment. The crowds around them became denser, so that they had to pay attention lest they bump into the people milling around the stalls. "You always know what you want, you don't seem to need a whole lot, you're bossy but in a way that doesn't make me feel dumb. Also, I think you're pretty funny."

"Funny?" Not once in Anah's entire life had she been called funny. No one laughed at her jokes because she didn't make jokes. Jokes were for Hailee and for Bucket. Jokes were for buffoons. Jokes were for people who didn't have a mission. "I'm not funny."

"Sure you are." Hailee moved ahead, creating a path that Anah was forced to follow until they came to a new stretch of road just wide enough so the two of them could walk abreast again. "You say really funny stuff. And, I guess I like how you react to things."

Affronted, Anah placed her hand on her chest. "What do you mean 'how I react to things'?"

Hailee chuckled. "Well, like yesterday, watching you with those kids? Golden."

Anah wanted to argue, but she wasn't entirely sure how to go about it. How could she argue about reactions she was having when she hadn't even been aware she was having them?

Once more, the smells from the spice stalls hit her nose, and she considered the bland food from the day before and those poor children, growing up thinking that vegetables were meant to be boiled, that meat was meant to be boiled... hell, that even the pudding was meant to be boiled. There were many other ways of cooking. Then she recalled Snoop and his mischievous delight at finding new ways to make her day harder. Maybe they just weren't to be trusted with fire.

It was no sooner than Anah and Hailee had reached the top of the temple stairs that the large, heavy doors swung open. Inside were two members of Farrow's local constabulary. Between them stood a very frazzled Pearl. The golden hair that had been so sleekly brushed and curled yesterday now frizzed in a halo around her head. The cool and contemplative eyes were bloodshot. And the lush mouth that Anah was sure Hailee was obsessed with was now pressed into a firm, thin line.

"I need you to get to the children now." Pearl said by way of greeting.

"Is everything okay?" Hailee asked, moving forward and placing a hand on the acolyte's shoulder. Anah winced, waiting for some sort of negative reaction. It didn't come. Instead, Pearl leaned into the touch. Two thoughts sprang into the forefront of her mind: that yeah, this was really happening, and that meant she would have to find a new partner. But also, a part of her was happy for Hailee, who never asked for anything and had always been generous with everything she owned.

"It's nothing for you to concern yourself with," Pearl huffed, though she seemed to soften with Hailee's nearness. "But I'm afraid I have important temple matters to deal with, and the children should not be left alone." As they started to head towards the door that would lead them to the school, Pearl tacked on, "In fact, it would be best if you made sure the children stayed tucked away today."

"Why's that?" Anah asked, feeling like the situation had gotten a lot stickier than it had been the day before, and that was saying something.

"Oh, just some things being misplaced inside the temple. Nothing large, but I don't want the children to draw the attention of the constables." Pearl's brows knit together. "I'm afraid, especially for Snoop, that there's not a lot of grace given to children. It's not fair and it makes me angry, but unfortunately the small are not always able to stand up for themselves."

Pearl's words may as well have been a knife spearing into her gut. Anah rubbed her chest absentmindedly, before shutting off the line of questioning that wanted to form in her mind. The line of questioning that asked, what if she had had someone like Pearl in her life instead of the people she'd had? What if she'd had an advocate instead of fear? She couldn't bother with any of that now. She was grown, it was done, and inside this temple somewhere was a halfling who had stolen something from her. Something that would make sure that the worries Pearl had for those children was something Anah would never have to concern herself with. Never again.

Pearl left them hurriedly, leaving Anah and Hailee to make their way to the classroom. Inside, it was chaos because of course. Snoop and Cheese were fighting, Cheese winning, but not by a lot. The twins had found the clothing for dress-up and were sporting some interesting combinations. Hope was sitting at the slate, drawing pictures of bodily anatomy that a six-year-old should not be aware of. And poor, poor Stevie was trying to sneeze into their elbow but only succeeding in burning their sleeve.

"Well, crap," Anah said.

# Chapter Fifteen

Anah surveyed the unstructured madness before her. Her shoulders sagged. Somehow, she was certain that it was just going to be a repeat of the day before. The kids lying, manipulating, refusing to listen, and being all around punks. She'd rather take on a blue dragon than attempt to keep these children in line. Before she could wallow too much, however, Hailee stepped forward.

"Shut it," she said, voice firm and commanding. Even Anah's spine straightened.

The room went still, all eyes locked on the monk. Hailee was wearing a sleeveless linen tunic, her well-muscled arms on full display. Around her hips sat her weapons belt—currently devoid of weapons, as (in theory, at least), she didn't need them in a classroom. Anah knew better than most, though, that Hailee's real skill was in fists and feet, her weapons more often for show than actual use. Her pants were loose and gauzy to allow for freedom of movement. Every inch of her looked capable.

"Everyone needs to sit in a circle now," Hailee said. Then almost as an afterthought, she added, "Please."

Anah stood, gaping. This couldn't be Hailee, could it? The same Hailee who laughed at her own farts, who challenged strangers to arm wrestling competitions, and who liked to walk on her hands when she got bored?

Yet the children moved quickly, settling into a circle around her. Hailee nodded in approval, and Anah could have sworn she saw something like admiration twinkle in Hope's eyes.

"Very good. We're going to try a new schedule today." Hailee scanned the room before catching Anah's attention, a smirk hiding in the corners of her mouth. Anah merely gestured, a sort of "after you" to imply Hailee had the floor. She might have been the assumed leader of their trio for several years, but part of being a leader was knowing when it was time to step back. *I'm not bossy*, she thought to herself, ignoring the strain the lack of control caused.

Hailee strode over to where the schedule had been posted. She ripped the parchment down, tearing it to small bits. This earned startled gasps from the children. Parchment was available, yes, but not cheap enough for it to be wasted.

"You can't do that!" Snoop cried, eyes narrowed. "Miss Pearl always tells us how expensive it is!"

Hailee only tossed the pieces of paper into an empty clay receptacle. Then she picked up the trash can, set it in front of Stevie, and said, "The next time you need to sneeze, buddy, aim it in here."

"Stevie ain't no buddy," Cheese said. "Stevie's just Stevie. They gets to decide if they want to be a buddy later."

Hailee apologized at once. "Sorry, Stevie. I won't do that again."

Stevie beamed, their tiny sharp teeth flashing, no offense taken. The smile held zero menace. In fact, it was downright delightful, and they flashed a clawed thumbs-up at Hailee. Anah stared in awe at the scene before her. This moment, in this classroom, somehow felt more magical than when she'd passed her magical apprenticeship.

"Hope, will you bring me the slate and chalk?" Hailee asked, now gentle.

The young girl swiped at her faucet of a nose with the back of her hand—gross—and did as Hailee requested. Supplies in hand, she marched to Hailee, handing them up in a reverent manner. Hailee smiled and nodded to where Hope had been seated. "Thanks. Go ahead and sit back down."

The children and Anah remained silent as Hailee held the slate up so she could erase pictures of anatomy that weren't remotely appropriate. The chalk squeaked as she wrote. Anah found she was holding her breath in anticipation just as much as the children were.

At last, Hailee rolled her shoulders back, cracked her neck, and turned the slate around so that everyone could see it.

# Schedule

1. Exercise
2. Circle time/learning
3. Make lunch, eat, and clean up
4. Rest time – books only, no toys
5. Chores-no setting things on fire
6. Play! (Anah found the exclamation point oddly

endearing.)

# 7. Dinner

"This is the schedule we'll follow for as long as Anah and I are your teachers," said Hailee. The children shared a quick look, and Anah couldn't decide if they were curious and questioning about the new schedule, or had picked up on the *"as long as"* addendum to Hailee's declaration.

It didn't matter because Hailee propped the slate up so it remained visible before gesturing that they should all stand.

"We're going to do some jumping jacks."

"Who's Jack?" Cheese asked, looking dubious.

"Why does he jump?" Snoop added on.

Stump looked hopeful. "Are we gettin' a new friend today?"

Hailee looked fit to split her seams. "You don't know what a *jumping jack* is?"

Anah decided not to chime in that she, too, was curious about Jack and his jumping.

"Nope," Hope replied. The others shook their heads.

"Push-ups?"

The kids shook their heads again.

"*Sit-ups!?*" Hailee's face was turning an alarming shade of red. Anah, at least, knew what these were. Anah placed her hand in front of her mouth to cover her smile. Her face muscles were beginning to ache from the frequent grins. When was the last time she'd ever smiled as frequently as she had since entering the temple the previous morning? Had she ever?

Hailee let out a sigh heavier than a pack ready for a seven-day hike. "Sheesh. Okay. Cool. We'll start with jumping jacks. Everyone follow me."

Hailee began to jump, her arms and legs spreading in an X as she did so. Then she jumped back, straightening into a pin. It took some awkward, bumbling tries for the children to catch on, but they did, and soon most were executing perfect jumping jacks. All, except for Stevie, who had to stop to rub their nose in an effort to prevent a sneeze.

After only ten jacks, Hailee paused, the rest of the children following suit, and turned her attention to Anah. "We're *all* doing exercise."

"You mean *all children* are doing exercise," Anah challenged. Exercise was not her forte. She could walk miles and... that was the end of it. She liked to think of her strength as coming in actions like firebolts and freezing spells and really anything, anything at all, that did not include working her muscles.

Hailee shook her head slowly, an ominous look forming on her face. "No, we're *all* participating." She cocked an eyebrow. "After all, we have to be good role models, don't we?"

Anah was going to kill her. She'd kill her later, maybe, while Hailee was sleeping. Or perhaps now was the time. Well, she would if she'd rested enough to manage a killing spell. But it was the tiny quirk at the corner of Hailee's mouth that sealed the monk's fate. She was doing this on purpose, the jerk.

"Fine." Anah grumbled and moved to the circle. Snoop and Cheese made plenty of room for her, so now she was among the children, feeling as if all teaching authority was being stripped from her. Assuming, of course, she'd ever had authority in the classroom to begin with. Worse, she was less than a head taller than the rest of the children. Gods, how humiliating.

Hailee picked up her count once more, all of them jumping, X-ing their bodies and back. It was a shamefully short time before Anah's heart was pounding in her chest and her legs began to feel a lot more like noodles than limbs. She really was going to have to have words with Hailee later.

"All right, everyone can stop." Hailee stood still, hands on hips, chest out, as proud as she could be. The children had little pink blooms in their cheeks. Or, in the case of Snoop with his stone-gray skin, a sort of purple. And Stevie, who was scaled.

"Now it's time for sit-ups."

Hailee lay on the floor and the children quickly followed suit. It wasn't until Hailee meaningfully cleared her throat that Anah grumbled and got into position with the rest of them.

"Remember not to pull on your neck," Hailee said, showing her hands laced at the nape of her hair. "When we do this, the tummy muscles are being used, like so." She rolled her body up, fluid and beautiful, like a wave cresting in the ocean.

The count began again. It was, Anah decided, a count marching them straight toward death by feebleness. Every time she managed to sit up, her muscles burned in panic, insisting she stop immediately because why? Just why?

She couldn't let the kids outdo her in something as simple as sit-ups, though, so Anah gritted her teeth and managed to keep up for the entire set.

When it was over, Anah almost collapsed, ready to weep in relief. That was, until Hailee cheerfully called out, "Time for push-ups!"

The kids were as happy as could be, eyes locked on the monk in admiration. A pang of envy managed to worm its way into Anah's still grieving midsection. It surprised her. She wanted them to look at her that way. Hailee's words from the previous night echoed in her head—the children didn't care about her heritage.

Before she could contemplate further, the pushups commenced. At least, for everyone but Anah. This time, it was not due to obstinance. Anah discovered that, for the life of her, she could not push herself off the ground. Her thin arms, capable of such destructive magic, refused to cooperate.

She heard Hailee's stifled chortle. "If you need to make it easier, you can put your knees down."

Stump yelled out, "Don't need to, Miss!"

"Yeah, don't need to!" came the reply from all the others, echoing Stump in delight.

This had Hailee absolutely losing it like a complete butthole, her body quaking while she continued to do push-ups with an ease that would put most athletes to shame. Anah did not find humor in the situation at all.

Cheeks burning with humiliation, Anah struggled to sit up. "My skills are in other places," she stated as she crossed her arms, which was difficult, since they weren't interested in responding at all.

When the exercises were finished, Hailee led them in stretches that Anah half-heartedly participated in, grumbling all the time. After finishing, Hailee clapped for them, clapped with actual enthusiasm, as if doing something as basic as exercise was worthy of praise.

*Let's see her call forth an infernal and bind it to her will. I'll be sure to let her know dropping to her knees won't make it any easier.*

Yet there was, beneath the prickling awareness of her weakness, a small sense of pride in having done most of the workout. And while every nerve in her body was a raging thread of agony, there was a rush of pleasurable relief Anah didn't get when casting a spell—not that she'd ever admit it to Hailee.

"That was a solid attempt, Miss Anah," Snoop snickered, clapping for her like she was a puppy who'd just attempted a delightful trick.

Hailee scooted out from the front, making her way to sit between Stump and Bruiser. "Okay, now Anah is going to teach us a lesson. We've entered 'learning time'".

Anah sat, stunned, just staring, mouth slightly ajar. Was she kidding? Was Hailee so rife with betrayal? First Bucket and now *this*?

Glowering, Anah made her way to the front, mind racing. "Can someone tell me what you've been studying so far?"

Snoop Dug raised his hand in the air. "I can, Miss, I can!"

"Snoop," Anah sighed, somehow unsurprised that the tiny gnome was the one volunteering information. Wasn't he the one who'd suggested the garden for chores the previous day? Anah decided to take anything he said with a grain of salt. She was suspicious that Snoop's motives didn't have her best interests at heart.

"We was learning about Dinna." He smiled wide, pleased with himself. "About how she likes growth and change and how she's gonna help us be better... " There was a smidgen of doubt in his voice at that last bit.

Anah held up her hand, signaling for silence. What was worse? That they were learning about a goddess without practical lessons as well? Or that they were being taught to depend on a goddess who represented things as nebulous and fickle as "growth" and "change"? What did that even *mean*?!

"Snoop Dug... how much do you know about the Underhill gnomes?" She wasn't remotely prepared to argue about the futility of hoping for change. Change was something you made for yourself. And growth? If Anah had figured that out, she wouldn't be so flipping pint-sized, now would she?

The poor gnome's face shuttered, locking down any exuberance that had been there. "Don't know much."

"Cheese? How much do you know about the ornwas?"

Cheese stretched, her fingers flexing, tiny claws peeking out from the tips. "Mmmm, I know enough. I know we're good at sneaking, and we're good at taking, and we're excellent at naps."

To be honest, that was about all Anah knew about the ornwas as well. She made a mental note to change that and research more later. When you were a mercenary, always on the road, it was best to know as much as possible about as many different folks as possible. Knowledge like that was good at aiding in negotiations or not saying something only to find oneself at the wrong end of a sword.

Anah looked at the twins next. "And you? What about your orc heritage?"

They shook their heads in tandem.

She shifted her attention to Hope. "And I suppose you at least know about humans?"

She had to, right? Humans made up the majority of Farrow. You couldn't throw a rock without hitting one of their stupid faces. While it was a hub for adventurers, adding a flavor of diversity, when it came to the day to day—the potion makers, the merchants, the cobblers, the tailors... most were human. Anah had always assumed that this was because most humans were fairly feeble.

Which, after that punishing exercise routine, she understood was ironic thinking. Hailee, with her beefy biceps and performance-worthy martial arts, seemed more the exception than the rule.

Hope only shoved a finger up her left nostril, causing a shudder to ripple down Anah's spine. She shut her eyes tight against the assault of that image, but nope... it was seared into her mind.

"I think this shows we should learn about ourselves first before focusing on deities." She gestured to the children. "Knowing who you are is important because then you know your strengths."

"And weaknesses," Snoop muttered, looking peeved.

Anah nodded. "You're right. It is especially important to understand weaknesses as well. How else will you guard against them in the future?"

At that, every single pair of underage eyes were locked on her, interest bubbling within. Pride flushed through her. Anah didn't need rippling abs to impress. Of course, she was only impressing a bunch of kids, but still.

Snoop only snorted. "S'pose you know lots about yourself, then?"

Anah knew she was being baited. Nonetheless, she decided to bite. "I do, in fact, know my heritage, dearest Snoop Dug." She folded her hands into her lap. "I'm what is called 'fell-touched'. Do you know what that means?"

Hailee started to speak, possibly in protest, but Anah shot her a silencing look. This was something Anah had learned to bear long before she'd met up with the monk. Hailee often witnessed the prejudice and misunderstandings Anah dealt with, but they didn't ever talk about how Anah felt regarding the demonic part of her blood.

"You've got horns." Hope managed to say this without needing to remove her finger.

It was the same observation she'd made the day before. Anah managed to swallow down the weary sigh that desperately wanted out. "Yes. As established yesterday, I do have horns. And yes, that is because I'm fell-touched. This means a human—my mother, in this case—had a child with a demon, like my father."

As soon as she spoke, Anah wished she had time-turning magic so she could wheel it back and not start this conversation. Her guard had dropped and she'd told them about her dad. About being part demon. Now she braced herself for the horror the children would certainly feel.

They would assume the weorst. Because demons were associated with, well, being pretty awful. So if she was part demon, she too must be...

Yeah.

"Did they love each other?" Cheese asked. She'd stopped grooming herself and was staring intently at Anah, who had to roll the question over in her head a few times. Nothing about evil, or black magic, or taking souls? Cheese wanted to know if her parents had been in love?

For a moment, Anah feared deeply she might get choked up. She hadn't cried in front of Hailee or Bucket, even with long years on the road, and damned if she was going to cry now. But Cheese's question was shaking her to the foundation. "That... " she cleared her throat. "I'm not sure. They didn't talk much about feelings."

"But they made a baby." This was Bruiser, who straightened up, quite pleased he could contribute to the conversation. "I know how babies are made. A man has to take his pen—"

"Just because you have a baby doesn't mean you share feelings," Anah hurried out, not wanting to open up a kind of lesson she was not prepared to give anyone. Ever. "Sometimes it's happenstance, or you had things in common, or... well, families can be made up all kinds of ways. Sometimes it isn't even by blood, but who you choose to love."

"So they did love each other?" Hope's poor brow was critically scrunched up.

"I doubt it." Anah paused, choosing the next words carefully. "They had things in common."

"Like what?" Cheese was leaning forward, fully invested now.

Anah shifted, uncomfortable. "My mom was a necromancer—"

"What's a necromancer?" Hope asked. Always Hope with the hard questions.

Hailee was shooting her a sort of ABORT ABORT ABORT signal, but Anah didn't know how to get off the conversation she'd started. "A necromancer is a person who uses their magic for more... dead body things."

"Like what?" Anah might need to do a silencing spell on Hope if she was going to keep peppering Anah with questions.

"Raising the dead is the basics, and it can go from there."

Hope giggled and rolled her eyes. "That's silly. Hailee's strong, I bet she can raise up lots of dead people. Maybe even throw 'em, too."

Wow, that wasn't... Anah pinched the bridge of her nose. "Anyway, my mom didn't want to just hang with reanimated bodies, so she decided to try and channel an infernal for conversation."

She'd actually wanted to kill the infernal then raise it as a thrall, but it hadn't worked out that way.

The children nodded as if this made complete sense. Hailee buried her face in her hands.

"She was sort of successful. She summoned a demon—my dad—instead of an infernal. Which is actually quite impressive, if you think about it, since infernals are lesser demons—"

The kids' eyes were starting to glaze over and Snoop started fake snoring. Anah huffed in irritation. "Fine. She summoned and bound my dad, and while I'm sure she didn't mean to get a baby out of the deal, here I am."

The irony, Anah knew, was people were concerned with her father and his side of the family. But if you asked her, the one to worry about was the one willing to attempt to enslave an infernal. It's not like Anah's mom was aiming for someone to help around the house. That was a maniacal, destroying-cities kind of goal.

"That's not a very good love story," Cheese said, sitting back in disappointment.

"I never said it was a love story. It's just my heritage. And because I know about both humans and demons, I know my strengths. Fire, as you saw yesterday. It takes a long, long time and a very hot fire for the flames to hurt me. Magic and spell work come more easily to me. I might be small, but Hailee will tell you I am capable of mighty things."

They craned their heads to look to Hailee, who verified it was true with a double thumbs-up.

"So what're yer weaknesses?" Snoop eyed her carefully, daring Anah not to share. To be fair, she didn't want to. She'd spent so much of her life trying to prove herself that admitting any vulnerability felt like a taboo. But they were kids, and, well, she found that she didn't mind all that much.

"My demon blood means I can tap into magic and cast without always needing regents or spell scrolls—I find those helpful but not necessary. But the human part of me means I eventually run out of that magic. Unless I can rest—we're talking deep, long sleeps over the course of a few nights—and drink some fell water, then I don't have much access to magic. And it gives me a wicked headache."

"Like yesterday!" Hope squealed in delight at the connection she'd made.

"Yep. Like yesterday. And today. I'm honestly quite tapped right now."

Cheese sprawled on her side, propping her head up on her hand. "How come your mom didn't teach you how to not run out of magic? Since she was so strong?"

An old wound split open. Not large enough to hemorrhage, but enough to weep bitterness into Anah's body. "My mother was good at magic but not good with children. And my father couldn't raise me in his hellscape because then I'd never be accepted in Deladrin at all. So, I found myself at a temple like this one, only at that one the parents don't come back."

Grief pierced her for only a moment before Snoop scooted across the woven rug and gently patted her knee. A painful lump lodged in her throat, and Anah swallowed hard. Perhaps opening up to Hailee had been like popping a cork—now her insides seemed desperate to spill out no matter how much she wished she could bottle it back up.

"It was cool how you walked through the fire yesterday," he said. "Super cool."

"Thanks, Snoop." Between the reassuring pat and this generous compliment, Anah wondered if Snoop had been abducted in the night and a changeling left in his stead.

The moment hovered, teetering like a troll with a stumped toe, and Anah wasn't sure if she wanted to stay in it or run away like hell. She'd shared slivers of her inner self with only two people in her life, and now she was in danger of being seen—truly seen—by a bunch of kids.

Before she could grow fully terrified of that understanding, Hailee's stomach rumbled loud enough that everyone sat up straight.

"Time for lunch?" she asked, a blush creeping up her brown cheeks.

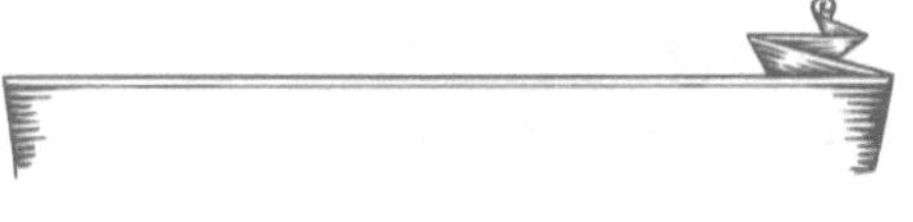

# Chapter Sixteen

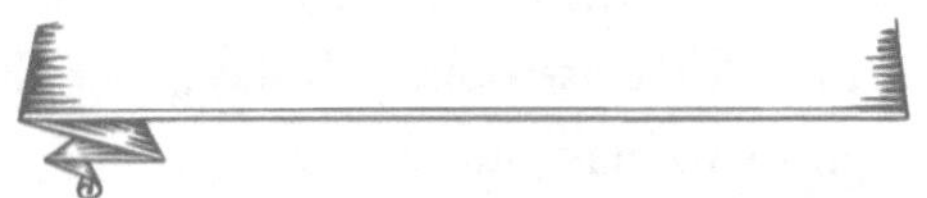

After sharing so much, Anah was desperate for a moment to collect herself. It didn't seem to be in the cards, though. "Who usually prepares lunch?" she asked, so she'd know who to talk to about the bland dishes.

"Miss Pearl does, but she starts cooking in the morning so it'll be ready by lunch," Cheese replied. "There should be something going already."

Anah grabbed at the opportunity for a second of privacy. "I'll go see what's on the menu."

Grateful, she hurried to the kitchen, only to discover it in a worse state than it had been the day before. Dirty dishes sat in rank stacks, the fire in the cooking hearth was more coals than anything, and the large copper pot hanging over it was empty of food but crusted within.

Disaster.

Anah's first impulse was to march to Pearl's office and ask what they should do, but she stopped. This was probably the exact sort of situation that had overwhelmed the acolyte to begin with. Furthermore, the way Pearl had greeted them that morning suggested she had neither the time nor patience for something so basic. It was just a kitchen and food, and Anah was familiar with both. This didn't have to be a kitchen calamity. It could be just another...

Quest.

Quests were something Anah could work with.

"We have a new mission," she announced grandly as she waltzed back into the classroom. "Today..." Anah paused for effect. "We're going to make lunch ourselves."

Cheese groaned loudly and the twins appeared to panic. Hailee grew stormy—she always did get hangry too fast—and Hope was too busy playing with her toes to listen to Anah. Snoop, of course, was the first to voice his protest. "Why should we?"

Anah smirked. She'd expected this reaction. "Because you're capable. Being able to feed yourself is a necessary skill and all of you are old enough to learn." Testing a hunch, Anah added, "And it will help Miss Pearl out tremendously."

Just as she'd hoped, Snoop's eyes grew luminous and hopeful at the opportunity to help out Miss Pearl.

Not wanting to give them time to doubt, Anah said, "Follow me to the kitchen."

Once everyone had filed in, the kitchen felt much tighter than it had before. Thank goodness the children were so small. "Hailee, you're in charge of finding the ingredients. Snoop and Cheese, you're in charge of chopping and cutting up anything that needs it. Bruiser, Stump, Stevie, and Hope can all scrub dishes so we have suitable tableware."

Hailee cleared her throat and whispered, "Are you sure you want to give them knives?"

"I think they can handle it." But remembering how experienced Hailee was with the children and how fish out of water she herself was, Anah tacked on, "Do you think they can handle it?"

Her friend shrugged. "Guess we'll find out."

Sudden visions of sliced body parts and Snoop's maniacal laughter flooded Anah's mind. She shook her head to clear it. "While you get lunch sorted, I'm going to go find out about a library."

It was the kids. They knew so little about the world and, while Dinna was pleasant enough to look at and apparently distant enough to allow someone like Anah into her sanctum, that wasn't going to cut it as an education. Pearl said to keep them alive. That wasn't going to be enough for Anah.

At least not while she was there.

The children needed access to reading and the acolyte would know how to make it happen.

As she wandered, Anah looked around for clues that Bucket was skulking about. She peered into doorways, finding small storage areas, chamber-pot rooms, and bathing rooms. No Bucket—not that he'd just be hanging about in the open—but Anah tracked all the dark corners and made a tally of things he'd need.

In one hallway, her shoes began to stick. Kneeling, Anah felt the surface of the stone walkway. It was tacky. She wrinkled her nose and stood, giving up on her search. This wasn't the way to find her quarry.

She discovered Pearl pacing and mumbling in her office. The door was open, but Anah felt as if she was wedging into a miasma of anxiety. "Is everything okay?" she asked.

Pearl startled at her voice. "Oh!" The woman pressed her hand over her heart. "You scared me."

Anah studied Pearl more closely. Her skin was paler, and there was some red in her sclera. Her robes were wrinkled, and Pearl just seemed ragged. "I thought the point of hiring us was to make things less stressful on you."

Pearl's laugh was strained. "Oh! Yes. Sorry." She absentmindedly started to comb through her long hair, trying to tame the frizz and fluff out lank locks. "You're right. It's not you. Well, that's not entirely true."

Anah went still. "Are we doing something wrong?"

"No! Probably not. Are you?"

Anah was stumped. Clearly something was stressing Pearl out, but if there were clues being dropped about what, Anah wasn't picking up on them. She wished people could just say what they meant so she didn't have to struggle so hard to parse it out.

Maybe that was why she'd stuck with Hailee and Bucket for so long. They knew her well enough she never had to guess at their needs. *Except Bucket had kept the part of him that was ready to betray me hidden.* Her heart refused to let go of the hurt and she despised herself for it. She wished she could cut it out like diseased flesh.

"I don't think so." *Aside from lying about why we're here.* "What's the matter?"

Pearl's shoulders slumped. "It's the thing from this morning. There are things going missing from all over the temple. I've been scrying to try to find out who is taking it, but every time I think I'm close to seeing someone, the vision gets wobbly and thick. There's a lot of pressure from the Elders to figure it out, though."

Bucket. It had to be. The little thief wasn't just taking from her, but from the temple of Dinna as well.

Except that didn't make sense to Anah. Bucket had always spoken of Dinna with reverence. It was hard to imagine he was creeping about, taking things for days on end. But if not that, then where were the items going? What was he *doing*?

Anah had a choice. She could tell Pearl about her true reason for being in the temple and offer assistance to help find Bucket. But she suspected that Pearl wouldn't be happy to discover her new teachers hadn't been there to help all along. She might even call the guard. Hailee's crush was growing exponentially by the day, and if Anah said something now, her friend's heart might be broken.

On the other hand, if she told Pearl now, the acolyte could nail down his location and she and Hailee could grab the wand and get out. The power Anah had wanted so desperately was almost within reach. Just one scrying pool away.

It should be an easy choice.

Steeling herself, Anah started. "You should know—" but the rest seemed to stick in her throat.

Pearl's eyebrow raised. "I should know what?"

The plan had been to just steel herself and get it over with. But Anah found herself hesitating and unsure. "That maybe the kids could help. You could turn it into a game of hide and seek."

Inside, Anah was berating herself. What was *that*?!

Pearl cracked a smile, though, easing some of the worry that had been etching itself into her face. "While that's a lovely idea, I don't think we should. We don't know if the thief is dangerous. If anything, I've been agonizing over whether we should close the crèche until they're found."

Which would mean what, exactly, for Anah? She knew better than most how skilled Bucket was at evasion. Would she and Hailee still have access to the inner parts of the temple? Or would they be expected to wait at the inn until Bucket was desperate to be let out?

"Don't cancel just yet." Anah tapped a finger thoughtfully against her lip. "Hailee is one of the best at protection and defense."

Pearl's lips pulled tight. "Is this from your previous...occupation?"

Anah worried the reminder that they weren't, in fact, in childcare might make things worse. In this case, however, it might be to their benefit. She'd have to trust in Pearl, a near stranger, which was a monumental challenge.

"Yes. She's most definitely the muscle of our group."

It was then that some color finally returned to Pearl's face in the form of a deep blush. "Is that how she manages to stay so... so... in shape?"

The situation would be a riot if it wasn't so critical that Anah keep it together. Of course the acolyte was just as interested in Hailee. Anah didn't understand the monk's magnetic charm, nor did she need to. She swallowed a chuckle and managed a nod.

"Well. I won't cancel yet, then. But the safety of the children must be your top priority. Things going missing is worrisome enough. I can't bear to think of one of them going missing."

"Of course." Anah witnessed the worry and the relief that Pearl wrestled with. The acolyte had spent a lot of time with the children and, whether difficult or not, had clearly come to care for them deeply.

Pearl sank into a chair, rubbing her temples. "I'm sorry. I've been rambling about my problems and forgotten to ask what it was you needed."

"What?"

"You came here for something, right? What can I do?"

Anah's brain waves clicked back into place. The kids. Reading. That's why she'd searched Pearl out. "I was wondering if there was a temple library? A scroll room or something? The class has decided to investigate reading and research, and it would be a good place for them to start learning."

The twist of Pearl's features wasn't one Anah was familiar with; she couldn't guess what was on her mind. But eventually the acolyte landed on a neutral face. "We do, but I'm not sure I'm comfortable with them in there."

"Because?"

Pearl ticked off on her fingers. "Well, Hope, for one, typically always has sticky hands. She could touch the parchment or scrolls and leave permanent marks. Then Cheese and Snoop, sweet as they are, tend to have more... figurative sticky fingers. I wouldn't put it past them to sneak something out. Stump and Bruiser are quiet and calm enough to be in the room, but they're still learning about their strength. It would be too easy for them to damage something important without meaning to. And Stevie..." Pearl offered a helpless shrug.

Anah felt a stone settle in her stomach. "Stevie *what*?" She had an inkling that she knew what Pearl would say. Anah refused to let her off the hook.

"He's prone to setting things on fire." Pearl at least appeared chagrined.

Too dirty. Too untrustworthy. Not able to control oneself. Combustible.

These were all things that had been hurled at a young Anah as reasons why she needed to be isolated. Why she didn't learn any real skills until she was out of the orphanage. And they were why the Wand of Birramos held so much appeal, because once it was hers, she wouldn't have to hear any of that ever again.

"Have you tried it with them?" She pushed Pearl, feeling bold with a long-suppressed anger born from injustice.

The acolyte grew flustered. "Well, no, but—"

"Just like the spices, right?"

Pearl's mouth opened and shut.

Anah took a deep breath, willing herself to calm down. If she started to smoke now, any points she wanted to make on the children's behalf would be rendered moot. "You were working alone for a long time. I'm not blaming you. With so many different personalities and needs in one class and just you to keep them safe, I know you made do with what you had. But if they don't learn now, their first steps in adulthood will be mired with simple failures that could have been avoided. They're old enough to do chores, to handle scrolls and texts, to try new flavors, to make themselves food—"

There wasn't a chance to keep the list going because Pearl launched out of her seat and began to push past Anah. "I forgot to make them lunch!" The guilt in the woman's tone softened Anah's irritation.

"That's okay, Hailee's there."

"The children are alone while Hailee cooks?" Pearl's fear rapidly swung to anger. "And you're here? That's so irresponsible—"

Anah held up a hand. "Let's go have a look, shall we?"

While her eyes remained narrowed, Pearl allowed herself to be led back to the kitchens. The sounds of laughter and the clatter of pots found them first, and Anah said a silent prayer to whoever was listening that they weren't about to walk in on chaos or dismemberment.

As soon as they stepped through the door, Anah relaxed. The scene before her was even better than expected.

Hailee was with Bruiser and Stump at the hearth, showing them how to add things to the enormous copper pot hung above. Stevie was squatting below them, gently breathing fire on the wood chips, keeping the smoke going and the heat evenly distributed.

Hope sat in a corner, humming to herself as she shelled beans. To Anah's relief, her face and hands were currently free of yuck.

Then there was Snoop and Cheese, each with a large knife in hand. As she and Pearl looked on, they chopped vegetables with slow precision before moving the chunks to a large stoneware bowl. They also snuck bites, popping pieces of vegetables in their mouths.

Cheese's tail was moving happily back and forth.

Pearl seemed too stunned to move, so Anah put a gentle hand on her shoulder to turn the acolyte around. "See?"

Pearl's eyes were growing shiny with tears. She grasped Anah's hands in hers, squeezing them. "I never dreamed they could do any of that! And none of them are complaining, either." Disbelief clung to every word. But also absolute rapture. "I'd hoped just to offer them a safe place, but this... teaching! It's a miracle."

"Not a miracle, just help. Like you said, there are two of us. And we're only having to take care of the children. So, maybe we can expect a bit more out of them. Change and growth, you know?"

Never mind that Anah still didn't buy into Dinna's whole thing, nor that she and Hailee weren't only here to take care of the kids. In fact, the children still came second to finding Bucket and getting back what was hers. She needed to remind herself of that priority.

But what was wrong with making sure she wasn't leaving the children or Pearl in a complete lurch once she'd achieved her goals? Anah could get what she needed and not be a complete jerk about it.

Pearl wiped away the tears threatening to fall before pulling her shoulders back and becoming the confident acolyte Anah knew her to be.

"Okay," she said with resolve. "I'll show you the library."

# Chapter Seventeen

Pearl had stayed to eat with the children. Anah witnessed how quickly the stress that had bound the acolyte's body fell away by the end of the meal. It had probably helped that the children had tried almost everything they'd cooked and, while not always fans, there'd been minimal complaining.

That was, until Anah announced it was time to clean up. Apparently, there was a limit to what they wanted to assist with.

"But it's rest time," Snoop countered slyly. "We needs our sleep and reading."

"Ah, but you don't have anything to read yet." Anah put her hands on her hips and enjoyed looking down at the gnome. It occurred to her that once she had the wand and was out of the temple, her days of being taller than someone would be over again.

Noses wrinkled in distaste, but Hailee flexed her large biceps and all the children quickly shushed, bizarrely entranced. Anah shook her head. "But if you do a good job and don't complain, I have a treat for you."

Hope's eyes grew large and round. "Is it pudding?"

"Uh, no."

Thin shoulders drooped. "Rats."

Anah bit back a laugh. "Miss Pearl said we can venture to the temple library. I can help you find some scrolls or books to read—carefully—during rest time." She chanced a look at Pearl, hoping the woman hadn't changed her mind.

When Pearl nodded, all the children cheered. That was all it took to get them up and scrubbing. The washing up took less time than Anah anticipated as every child dedicated themselves to the tasks given to them. Impressed, Anah and Hailee had them line up to follow Pearl.

Aside from some small whispers from the children, they were on their best behavior. Anah imagined this was due to being allowed to try something new and not wanting to screw it up.

Finally, they reached the temple's library. Windows lined the tops of the walls, allowing natural light to spill in over a few desks and chairs in the middle. A surprised acolyte looked up when they entered, his face blanching as the children spilled in. Anah didn't blame him. Though tremendously smaller than the Academy libraries in the larger cities in Deladrin, it was impressive for a temple devoted to one of the lesser deities. Scrolls were stacked in neat rolls along shelves. Sheaths of papers bound with twine were available as well. And books, their leather-bound covers in rich colors, lined an entire back wall.

Pearl turned to face them. There was no missing the renewed panic in her expression, but she managed a tight smile. "There are rules. Acolyte Thomas can help you find reading suitable to your age and reading level, as well as interests. He will also explain how to handle what you borrow."

A squeak pulled her attention to Thomas. His cheeks quivered as he meekly asked, "Borrowing?"

There was a shared moment of hesitation between the two. To Anah's relief, though, Pearl doubled down. "Yes, borrowing. Obviously nothing too priceless or valuable. Now, I'm afraid I must leave."

Before Thomas could argue, Pearl swooped out, her robes billowing as she exited. It wasn't until she'd completely disappeared that Anah realized she should have asked for more clarity on the definition of "priceless or valuable."

For a moment, Thomas appeared to prepare to bolt after Pearl. Hailee slung an arm over his shoulders, though. "Okay, Thomas. Have you met the kids?"

His throat bobbed as he swallowed, shaking his head. Vaguely, Anah recalled how terrified she'd been when first seeing the children. The poor guy was just being confronted with something new.

"I'm going to point to each of you one by one," Anah stated firmly. "Thomas will help you each find something to borrow. Until then, I need you to sit, hands in your lap. Not your nose, Hope."

The little girl only smiled.

They all did as instructed, though their excitement was palpable. Stump and Bruiser were rocking with energy, while Cheese's tail flitted nervously.

"Stevie." Anah pointed. Then, to Thomas, "Do you have anything regarding dragonlings and allergies?"

For a stunned moment, Thomas was so rigid Anah prepared to repeat herself. But then the acolyte got himself together. He quickly went to a shelf with a collection of slim volumes and scrolls. At first, he picked up one of the rolled pieces of parchment. But after a second glance at Stevie and their twitching nose, opted for a thin, leather-bound book instead.

Stevie smiled as they took their prize back to the group. Snoop reached out to grab it, but the dragonling clutched it to their chest like it was treasure. Which, Anah supposed, it might be. Either way, she hoped there was something in there to help with his sneeze attacks. Once those were gone, Stevie could work on controlling his fire.

Hope went next, receiving a sort of manual on monsters, with gorgeous sketches accompanying many of the listings. While she could read, some of the finer calligraphy made sounding out words difficult. The pictures, though? They were exquisite. Anah made a mental note to peek over her shoulder.

Stump asked for something about flowers, to Hailee's delight. Thomas handed him an introduction to botany scroll. Bruiser, on the other hand, wanted a cookbook. The poor acolyte had to scrounge for that. Apparently the library of Dinna didn't contain many cookbooks. Considering Pearl's reluctance to change routines, this was both humorous and ironic.

When Thomas started to hand Cheese a history of ornwas, she made to grab it with her claws out, a cheeky grin on her furry face.

"Put them away," Anah ordered. "If you return it with so much as a single puncture mark, you lose borrowing abilities for six months, Cheese."

The cat-girl sighed as melodramatically as possible before the claws disappeared into the tufts of her fingers. She wiggled her paws to show her restraint.

When it was Snoop's turn, however, Anah chose for him. "Something in ancestry," she said, tapping her lip with a thoughtful finger. "The Underhill gnomes."

At first, the young gnome balked while Thomas rushed to find something, probably eager to get all of them out of his library. "I can pick out me own book," he argued.

"Yes, but I think you'll benefit from this one." She bent at the waist to so she was eye to eye with him. "Just because the Underhill gnomes chose to miss out on your genius doesn't mean you have to miss out on your history. You understand? They don't get to decide who you are. You do."

Snoop wiped hard at his eyes. "Stupid library's full of dust," he complained, voice rough. "And I hear you."

Thomas returned slowly, a thick book bound in fine leather with gilded lettering in his hands. "This is what we have, but..."

Anah crossed her arms. Hailee moved into place behind her, turning them into a wall of menace. "But what?" Anah asked, ice in her voice.

"It's rare and rather expensive."

This was a situation where Pearl being more specific would have come in handy. "Is there anything else? Even if it isn't as specific?"

Thomas's face paled, a sheen of sweat glistening. "No. There aren't many Dinna worshippers amongst the Underhill gnomes, so we didn't try to collect much."

Anah turned to Snoop Dug, who was beginning to show the signs of grave disappointment. She knew what he was thinking. That once more he was being overlooked because of who he was. "He can borrow it."

Thomas gawped. "But Acolyte Pearl—"

"Trusts him. And I do as well."

As she said it, Snoop Dug shot her a look so heart-wrenchingly full of hope that Anah's breath hitched. So when Thomas didn't make to hand it over to the gnome, Anah allowed her skin to begin to smoke with genuine irritation. It didn't matter if people were cruel through ignorance. Cruelty remained what it was: harmful.

Thomas caught a whiff of the smoke and immediately thrust the tome into Snoop's thin arms and pointed to the door.

Anah was happy to oblige.

As they made their way back, Hailee offered to carry the large, heavy book for Snoop. But he clutched it tight and shook his head. Anah monitored each child and saw the reverence with which they studied or held their reading materials and knew she'd done something right.

She hadn't profited from the gesture, and yet she'd done it anyway. And she *still* managed to feel good regarding her choice. Strange. *Unnatural*, she tried to convince herself. The thought evaporated almost as quickly as it had formed.

In the room, there was almost complete silence as the children set out their cots and crawled onto them, absorbed in their reading. Well, except for Hope, who wanted to show everyone each new illustration she found.

Hailee leaned in. "That was kind of you."

Anah's back stiffened. "I don't know what you're talking about." This earned her one of Hailee's pointy elbows in the ribs. "It's not a big deal," Anah amended in a whisper. They were just books.

"What prompted the field trip?"

Now Anah stared daggers at her friend, hoping the monk would get the hint. "I wanted further access in the temple. To look for Bucket. Unless you forgot why we're here?"

Hailee's easy smile said volumes about what she was thinking. "Funny. I almost worried the same was true of you."

How *dare* she! "Take it back or I will turn everything you love into ash."

Hailee choked back a laugh. "You'd have to include yourself in that, then, dummy, as I'm pretty fond of you."

Anah sputtered, not knowing how to handle that pronouncement. "First you want to talk about my past and now you're getting gushy. Stop it right now, Hailee, or I'll make you regret it."

"Pretty sure you still don't have enough magic to do that yet. Are you going to spark me to death?"

Anah imagined knives hurtling from her eyes, stabbing straight into Hailee's chest. Sitting, Anah drew her knees to her chest and rested her chin on them. They'd been in the temple for only two days and yet Hailee's observation was closer to the mark than Anah liked. There were increasing stretches of time where she forgot why she was there, too focused on the children.

"How are we going to find him?" Hailee's voice had dropped further, but she shouldn't have worried. All eyes were still glued to the reading materials. Hope's were beginning to flutter shut as the need to nap grew impossible to resist.

"I'm not sure. Being in charge of these creatures has put a limit on how much we can search. I'm still recovering my magic, so that's a barrier as well."

"Oh. Cool." Then, "So, we just wait until he's done hiding out?"

"I don't think so. Pearl was stressed this morning because things are disappearing from all over the temple. I'd wager Bucket's gathering supplies. When he tries to leave, he'll be in for a surprise. He'll come to us."

"How will he know we're here?"

"He probably already knows. You know how good Bucket is at reconnaissance. When he understands there are no other options, he'll reveal himself."

Hailee stretched, cracking the bones in her neck. "You know what's been bothering me? Why a temple?"

Anah's brows pressed tight together. "I haven't got a clue. Which," she admitted, "is driving me more than a little crazy."

Hailee patted her on the head, right between the horns. "You were already there, Boss."

# Chapter Eighteen

S *luuuuuuuuuuuuuuuuuuuuuuurp.*
Wobble.

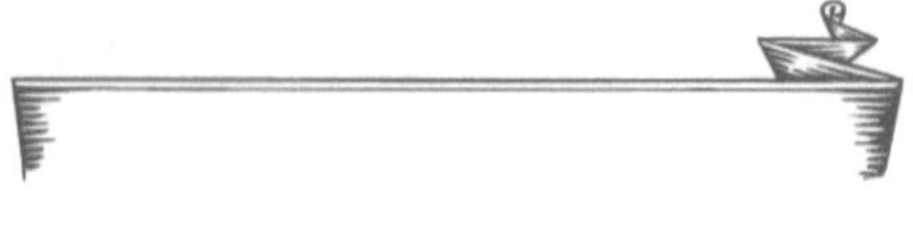

# Chapter Nineteen

It was the biggest book he'd ever seen—not that he'd had opportunities to look at books much.

Snoop dared a peek at the two teachers. Their heads were close together, faces masks of frustration. Only a day or two ago, he would've assumed they were irritated at the children. Or more specifically, him, because it was almost always him the grownups got mad at.

But the weight of the tome in his lap made him think otherwise. Miss Anah had arranged for them to go to the library. She'd convinced Miss Pearl and that other acolyte that they could borrow the books!

And she'd said she trusted him.

Snoop Dug wasn't used to adults trusting him, and he discovered that he liked how it felt when one did—especially one as grouchy as Miss Anah, who didn't seem to like or trust in much at all. That made her vouching for him *mean* something.

It was this line of thinking that had him reading the same paragraph over and over. It wasn't that the words were too hard to read, but that his brain wanted to remind him of the fertilizer stink bombs. One of which was hiding in one of the main vents leading into the classroom. Just thinking about it made his tummy hurt.

He'd made them on the day of the Great Garden Distraction, barely managing to get the components needed before the teachers had put out the fire. At night, he'd snuck out of his room to place them in various vents around the school wing of the temple, the idea being that whoever was sneaking around would trigger a stink bomb and be chased out by the smell, then be caught. Snoop Dug was a skunk, and he was going to mark the perpetrator.

But so far none had gone off, and Snoop Dug found himself doubting. Had he placed them in the wrong spots? Had he made a mistake in the bomb's design?

Glancing around, he noticed that everyone was reading except for Hope, who was sleeping, and the teachers—who were still whispering. As much as he'd adored the idea of stinking the culprit out, he had to presume his plan was a bust. He'd have to risk being caught at night again, this time removing all the bombs and finding a way to dispose of them. Except that left too much time to hope nothing triggered one.

He'd have to find a way during the school day.

Decision made, he tried again to tackle the history of his people.

It was no good. The words continued to blur in front of his eyes. It was agony to wait for rest time to be over. When the teachers finally stood and asked them to put away their cots, he raised his hand.

"Yes?" Miss Anah's eyes were a brilliant shade of red, making it impossible for him to know if she was upset with him or not. Honestly, he was jealous of them. How badass would it be to have crimson eyes?

"I was thinkin' for chores . . . we could clean the room?" That would give him plenty of time and distraction to get rid of the stink bomb.

"Not today, buddy," Miss Hailee answered instead. "Today we're helping clean Dinna's statue in the main part of the temple."

Snoop shifted his weight from one side to the other. He loved it when they were allowed out into the temple proper. It was so light and green and the best place to stare at people and dare Cheese to prank them. But he also needed to remove the bomb.

"I'm sure it's fine," he said. "'Sides, the room is getting sticky."

This, at least, was true. None of them knew why, but the surfaces of the tables, the toys, and even the floor were tacky. It confused him as, so far as he knew, none of them had done anything to make them so gross. Not even Hope, whose nostrils produced some super sticky icky.

"Perhaps we can do double the chores," Miss Hailee teased. "First the statue, and then the sticky classroom?"

At that, everyone—Snoop included—groaned. No *way*.

"We've been asked to help with the statue," Miss Anah added. "So it's kind of mandatory."

"What's mandatory mean?" Hope was playing with the hem of her shirt. At least she wasn't digging in her nose again. Once, Miss Pearl had discovered Hope's secret stash of boogers, all lined up on the wall. Hope had been using them like glue to hold up pictures she'd made.

That had been a bad day.

"It means we have to." Miss Anah pointed to the door. "Line up."

The authority in her voice should have rankled, yet Snoop found it comforting. The first day, Miss Anah had been so scared of them that any respect he would've had for a grown up evaporated.

But then she set herself on fire.

You had to respect anyone who'd self-immolate.

With one final, forlorn glance at the vent, Snoop went to line up with the others.

For the first time in memory, Snoop stuck to the task at hand. He wiped off the statue, aided in sweeping around the base, and helped to train some of the vines to grow up the right portions of the nearby walls. He couldn't afford to dawdle like he usually did.

Cheese sidled up beside him, her eyes slits. "What're you up to?" she whispered. "You're *helping*." She made it known how uncool that was.

"Remember when I needed to get into the shed?"

She nodded before anxiously licking a paw. Cheese didn't like being out in the open as much as he did. There weren't enough places where she could hide and, presumably, jump out to scare someone.

"I made something, um, explosive. And smelly."

Her tail twitched. "That sounds fun. So what's the problem?"

"Whoever's in the vents hasn't triggered them. But it isn't like I made them with stability in mind, you know?"

"Oh, Snoop." Cheese reached out to pat him on the head. "Well, at least you'll get rid of the new teachers when one of them goes *pop*. Then you'll have Miss Pearl back."

He wished he hadn't confided in Cheese about his plan to marry Miss Pearl when he got older. Now he wondered if he should admit to Cheese that he didn't mind the teachers quite so much anymore. She might tease him even more then.

Relief flooded through him when it was time to get back to the room.

That relief was short-lived, however. It started when Hope let out a shriek. Miss Hailee vaulted over several desks in a leap that would have been impressive if Hope's piercing cries didn't demand one's full attention.

"My blanket!" Hope's body quaked with the ferocity of her anguish. "My blanket's gone!" Everyone knew Hope's blanket was her most cherished possession.

This caused a panic among the others, who scurried to their cubbies. The twins immediately began to wail, each holding up a single shoe. They both screamed some variation of "One shoe is missing!"

Cheese was relieved upon discovering her cubby was untouched, and Stevie never kept much in their cubby anyway.

Anxious, Snoop checked his. He didn't keep much in it, but he'd stored the book there. The one the acolyte hadn't wanted to let him borrow. The one that had been entrusted to him.

His stomach plummeted when he peered in and discovered... nothing.

Heart pounding, he reached in, like maybe his eyes weren't working and his hand would discover the book sitting where he'd last left it. He didn't want to contemplate what would happen if it was gone. It was too awful. The only thing he touched was the base of the cubby and something goopy.

"Ew." Withdrawing his hand, Snoop rubbed his fingers together. They were covered in something pale and viscous, the sticky-smooth quality of it deeply unsettling.

But he was a gnome of science, and despite all the reasons he shouldn't, he brought the coated fingers up to his nose and inhaled.

It smelled sweet. Sweet?

There was a hint of vanilla to it, the sort of warm scent associated with pudding.

His tongue darted out, taking the tiniest lick. It *was* pudding.

The wheels and cranks in his brain started turning. Amid the cries of despair from his friends and the stained, desperate consolations of Miss Anah and Miss Hailee, Snoop processed his discovery.

Obviously the thief had come into their room to steal things. He'd overhead Miss Pearl worrying about stuff going missing all over the temple. The pudding, though...that had been the first thing to go missing, hadn't it? And he'd been the one blamed for it!

With hyper-focus, Snoop leaned in close enough to spot the smear of sweet that trailed out of his cubby. He could just make it out along the floor, though the wood was so worn from use he had to shift angles here and there to catch the sheen of it.

Sure enough, there were trails from each of the cubbies. From there, the trail led to the vent.

THE vent.

*Oh no.*

Snoop scanned the room. The twins were arguing over which of them would be able to wear both shoes and which would have to go without. They were starting to shove. Bruiser pushed Stump into one of the shelves and it rocked, threatening to tip over. Hope was inconsolable, her sobs so loud his ears hurt. Cheese was making it worse by trying to explain all the reasons why having a special blanket made Hope a baby, anyway, so she should be glad it got lifted. And Stevie? The dragonling was tucked in near Miss Anah, clutching at her skirt.

No one was paying attention to him. Snoop moved over to the vent. It connected to others within the temple and while he knew the idea was to help with airflow, he'd always thought they didn't do anything except invite small people to explore.

There was another gloop of pudding lining the edge. It had begun to drip down the wall. Biting his lip, Snoop reached in, searching carefully for his stink bomb.

*There.*

He picked the bomb up with utmost care, gagging at the slime of pudding coating the rough canister. Now he knew why it hadn't been triggered. The thief had used the pudding to cover the bomb, rendering it useless, before moving into the classroom to filch a drool-crusted blanket, one shoe from each of two pairs, and a rare tome about the Underhill gnomes.

Because you could do what, exactly, with all of that?

Whatever it was, Snoop had to do what he hated the most. He needed to ask for help, because there was no catching a criminal when he couldn't understand even a hint of their motives. Cradling the stink bomb in his hands, Snoop turned slowly, intent on telling Miss Anah everything.

But he found he couldn't. The words were just as stuck in his mouth as his feet seemed stuck to the ground. Over and over, his mind played a loop of "we trust him" and "rare and expensive" along with the fearful expression of Thomas the acolyte. Over and over.

He'd been in trouble so many times. His experiments, his curiosity, and his many mistakes had led to him carrying a reputation among the temple's keepers. It wasn't a reputation he was proud of, though he pretended he didn't care. Eventually, though, would his reputation outweigh Miss Pearl's attempts to keep him there?

Would it matter that he suspected he knew where the book had gone? That it wasn't his fault? Or would they take one look at him and blame him anyway, ruining any trust he'd built up with the teachers? He might lose his home.

The fear of losing that held him rooted in place, a statue on the outside and a riot of panic within. So when a tantruming Stump threw his other shoe, sending it hurtling straight at Snoop, he didn't react in time. Instead, he watched it turn toe over heel through the air until it struck him in the chest.

Hard.

The fragile, goopy canister in his hands slipped free and fell.

"Oh. My. Glop."

As soon as it hit the ground, it shattered. Snoop understood two important things in that moment. The first was that the explosive component had failed. The second was the stink factor had not. The stench slammed into his nostrils like a punch and he reeled back, eyes watering.

Soon, the shouts and cries in the room shifted from chaotic to unified. A sudden and intense row of *what is that smell?*

Miss Anah immediately immolated, small flames licking along her arms and legs. It appeared to be self-defense, because just after she looked down to Stevie, realizing how close the dragonling was to her, the fire disappeared as quickly as it had come. It was Stevie, though, and the small scales covering their skin were resistant to flames. The dragonling managed a small smile at Miss Anah before the smell ruined any hope of ever smiling again.

At least, that's how it felt to Snoop at the moment.

"Everyone out!" Miss Hailee shouted, pointing to the door that connected to the kitchen hallway. Everyone, Snoop included, began to run, needing to be away from the stink as soon as possible. "In a line, please!" she tacked on, but thankfully she didn't ask them to be slow.

Snoop's lungs felt heavy with grossness. His nose burned with the smell so much that his tongue seemed to want to join in on the fun, tasting as if coated in the vilest substance in the world. His stomach wanted to jump out of his throat and, based on the coughs and wails of his friends, they were in the same boat.

Miss Hailee led them out, half-jogging as they made their way to the garden. Miss Anah took up the rear, putting a reassuring hand on Snoop's shoulder when he stumbled. His skin burned where she'd touched him. Not due to Miss Anah's heat, but his own shame that scalded where her hand had been.

Fresh air was a blessing. Cheese, whose sense of smell was keener than most species, fell to her knees and began to scoop dirt onto her tongue, trying to scrub out the lingering foulness.

Chests heaved and tears flowed. The children dropped to the ground to sob, bodies exhausted. Miss Hailee bolted to the well and began to haul up water. Snoop assumed it was to drink until she upended the bucket over herself, rubbing furiously at her brown skin.

When the twins rushed to her, Miss Hailee helped them do the same. Her arm muscles banded and her skin shone in the sun as she worked with unbelievable speed and grace to give every child who came near a dousing.

Snoop dragged himself up. His eyes watered heavily, the wet tracking trails down his cheeks. He knew this was the last moment before everything changed, and he almost wished he could run back in and hide in the stink instead of facing the grownups.

Miss Anah moved next to him and offered him her hand. Snoop stared at it while a belt of anguish cinched tight around his chest. Mute, he shook his head. He made his way to the well and allowed the water to be dumped over him.

He wasn't sure how to ever feel clean again.

The doors flung open and several acolytes, including Miss Pearl, came hurtling into the garden courtyard, coughing and gagging. As soon as Miss Pearl saw the wet children there, her face blanched. When she homed in on Miss Anah and him, Snoop knew it was over. He braced himself for her wrath.

It wasn't Snoop that Miss Pearl unleashed on, though.

It was Miss Anah.

"What happened?" Miss Pearl was shouting, her anger bringing color back to her cheeks. "It's been two days! First the fire in the garden and now this?"

Snoop waited for Miss Anah to fire back. But the petite teacher had a resigned slump to her shoulders, like this was what she'd expected all along.

"I let you take them to the library! To borrow scrolls! Now I'm not sure if anything in this wing of the temple can even be salvaged!"

Over to the side, several of the acolytes were vomiting in the grass, the splatter decorating the hems of their brown robes.

Miss Hailee came over. Snoop witnessed a look of loss skirt across her features, like she thought she'd get to have pudding *and* cake but instead was having to choose vegetables. "Stop yelling at her," she ordered Miss Pearl.

It was the first time Snoop had heard anyone talk like that to Miss Pearl.

"Oh, I'm yelling at both of you." Miss Pearl stopped shouting then, choosing instead to growl. "I told you how stressed I am. How badly I needed help. Instead, you've made everything harder. Do you know the kind of trouble this has caused? What the temple elders might do?"

Forgetting that he should probably remain silent, Snoop blurted out, "What might they do?"

They all seemed to notice him there. Pearl's mouth pressed in a tight line. After a moment, she said, "They'll shut down the crèche. The parents will want their children far away from us, the funding will disappear, and the school will cease to exist."

Snoop felt his lower lip wobble. "Where would they go? Cheese and the twins and Hope and Stevie?"

Miss Pearl sighed. "Their parents will find other childcare. The Babysitters' Guild will have someone."

He was almost too afraid to ask, but he did. "And me? Where will I go?"

When Miss Pearl's voice cracked and she couldn't answer, he understood. He'd be homeless and alone.

"But that hasn't happened yet, Snoop." Miss Anah spoke softly. "No one has closed anything. Hailee and I will tender our resignation. Miss Pearl will be able to soothe the parents with our exit. Before I leave, I'll find a way to help remove the smell." She squatted to look Snoop in the eye. "You won't lose this," she assured him.

His eyes pricked. She had to know it was his fault. Yet Miss Anah was prepared to take all of the blame.

If he let her, Miss Pearl might never get angry with him. He'd done some bad things before, but this was definitely next level. At what point would Miss Pearl stop seeing him as someone worthy of helping?

But if he let Miss Anah do this, he'd never see her again. Miss Pearl would go back to being so frazzled she wasn't any fun. Most likely she'd bring in more new teachers and, if they were like the ones in the past, Snoop would waste no time trying to get them to quit.

Oh, how his heart hurt. He thought he might throw up, but Snoop turned to Miss Pearl. "Don't let her quit. Or Miss Hailee."

Miss Pearl's face twisted with compassion. "I'm sorry, Snoop, but they're at fault."

"No, they're not. It was me." Snoop dashed away the tears. He'd said it out loud and already felt stronger having the truth out. "I had Stevie set the garden on fire so I could get into the fertilizer shed. I took some stuff and used it to make stink bombs. When everyone was asleep in the temple, I hid them in the vents."

Pearl blinked several times, processing. Miss Anah eyed him, her face giving no clues as to what she was thinking.

Unable to stop himself, he kept talking. "Don't let them quit," he begged again. "It's not their fault I'm a bad kid."

Both adults softened at once. Miss Anah said "You're not a bad kid" with such vehemence it shook him deep inside. "Poor choices don't make you a bad person."

He moved before he could help himself, with no thoughts of the consequences. Snoop flung himself at Miss Anah, his arms wrapping tight around her waist and his face hidden in her chest. Miss Anah was warm and he didn't care if it was because she was fell-touched or just because he wasn't used to hugging anyone.

The contact would have been enough, but when he felt one of her arms drape over his shoulder, holding him, too, Snoop thought the perfect, lovely hurt of it might be the end of him.

Behind him he heard Miss Pearl's long, drawn out sigh. "Okay. We're going to need to talk about this later, Snoop."

It wasn't a conversation he looked forward to, but at the moment, he was as happy as someone who'd just drenched the temple of a goddess in near toxic stink could be. Miss Anah gently separated them. When he looked up at her, she was all business.

"Pearl, I don't suppose the temple has a secret cache of fell water?" Anah was rubbing her hands together. Small drifts of smoke curled up from between her palms.

"Um, no." Miss Pearl looked perplexed and genuinely remorseful. "How would that help?"

Snoop couldn't help it. With pride, he answered. "Miss Anah's fell-touched. But she needs the water and some rest to regain her magic. Right, Miss Anah?"

His teacher smirked at him. The sun caught a curve of her long, ivory and gray horns, making them look like they were glowing. "You got it, bud." She returned her attention to Miss Pearl. "I've got some reserves left in me, but I'm running low. I think I have enough to clear the building of the smell."

With that, his mistakes were pushed to the side, and the entire class plus Miss Pearl began to work on clearing the smell.

While he and the other kids always got along, this was the first time Snoop had experienced actual collaboration with them. Something felt different about not only *liking* his friends but actually doing something productive with all of them. It made the bonds between them feel stronger.

Snoop worked with Miss Anah, showing her how he'd made the bomb. Several times in his explanation she'd purse her lips or her brows would pinch, but occasionally he caught a nod of admiration. Once she understood the mechanics and the components used to formulate the awful, lingering stink, she told him she could craft a counter spell.

Miss Hailee showed them how to turn scraps of cloth into face masks and they practiced breathing through their mouths instead of their noses. Miss Anah handed them each items imbued with temporary magic. Since they were in the garden, these were mostly made up of garden tools.

Dressed for battle and armed with spades, the class made their way back into the temple. Stevie led the way, getting to practice his fire-spitting on purpose for the first time ever. He did so with gusto. Beside him came Miss Anah, continuously burning as she went. Cheese and Snoop went behind them, waving spades in broad circles and watching the magic shimmer in the air. They were followed by the twins, who clutched enormous fans that they pumped back and forth, creating movement in the air. Finally, Miss Hailee came last with Hope on her shoulders, the small child waving her garden stake at the ceiling to ensure none of the stench clung to the high, tight corners.

It took the rest of the day. The others' parents showed up and Miss Pearl had to both introduce Miss Anah and Miss Hailee while also explaining what happened. No one left happy.

By the end, the smell was gone and all that lingered was the burnt-wax smell of a candle that had recently been snuffed out. Miss Pearl was busy trying to smooth over things with the temple elders. Miss Hailee had to carry Miss Anah, who was soaked with sweat and had deep purple bruises of fatigue under her red eyes. It was difficult to see the teacher so worn out.

And Snoop had been forgotten, if temporarily, for the rest of the evening.

He was bone-tired from the day and soul-tired from the myriad of emotions he'd experienced. But Snoop knew he couldn't sleep. One problem had been solved, but he had a running list of things that had to be completed before the start of school the next day.

Despite knowing how much he risked by breaking rules yet again, Snoop set to it, determined to right his wrongs.

# Chapter Twenty

Magnus had only allowed them into the inn after Anah and Hailee had soaked in the back in heavily scented water, their clothing from the day scoured and hung to air dry outside. There'd been a slightly embarrassing moment when she and Hailee had to make their way through the main floor of the inn wrapped in bed linens, the patrons looking on in surprise as two nearly nude figures passed in their midst.

But now, upstairs and in bed, Anah stretched out under the sheets and stared at the ceiling, wanting nothing more than sleep. It didn't come, however. She had Snoop Dug on the brain, along with all the questions the small gnome brought with him.

Hailee was doing pushups. She must have been too wired for sleep as well. After a set, she squatted. "Anah?"

"Yeah?"

"I just... is this worth it? The wand, I mean. Is it worth all of—" Hailee gesticulated wildly with her hands to imply *all of this.*

Anah wasn't sure how to answer anymore. She hated it. Finally, she said, "I thought it was. The Wand of Birramos was designed by an infernal. It was a test of sorts. First one has to find the wand, which they had. Then she'd have search out a fell-stone jeweler, who would have cut the ruby. The ruby itself wasn't from their world, but from the eighth level of the hells. By cutting it and attuning herself to it, Anah would have a constant connection to the demonic powers of all the hells."

Hailee sat on the floor, legs crossed. "So, you'd never need the fell water or rest again?"

"I'd never need them again. The amount of magic I'd be able to do would be limitless, really."

"Why didn't you tell Bucket and me what you were after? I didn't understand that it was important to you and not just worth money."

Anah sat with that for a moment. "Because telling you would have meant admitting how weak I feel most of the time."

Her friend moved to sit on the other bed, facing her. Hailee steepled her fingers under her chin. "Do you truly believe you're weak? You're the only spellcaster I know with knowledge of multiple magic systems. You aren't bound by water, or air, or earth. Would a wand make that much of a difference? Why not just take better care of yourself?

If Hailee had asked those questions the morning they'd awoken to a missing Bucket, Anah wouldn't have thought twice before saying she deserved the power. Now though, she couldn't say what, exactly, she'd use all of it *for*. In an effort to avoid answering, she argued, "I take care of myself."

Hailee snorted. "Do you remember when we first met?"

Anah did. It was in a small town about a hundred miles southwest of Farrow called Glib. "I was trying to buy dinner and a drink."

"And the bartender insisted you were a child and needed to get out," Hailee added. "You were standing there, smoking in anger and about to burn the whole damn place down. So I pretended to be your coworker and assured him you could, in fact, drink. That's when you told me you'd forgotten to eat for too long and low blood sugar was exacerbating your temper."

It had been a miserable moment heaped on to a mountain of miserable moments in Anah's life. She'd only just been released from her sorcery apprenticeship and had been trying to find work. Everywhere she went, they turned her away because they either didn't believe she was old enough or they didn't trust a fell-touched. "You had to sit with me then, to sell the story. That's when I found out you'd left the monastery and wanted to see the world."

"And you needed work. So we got work. Together."

It had started as small and odd jobs. Whatever they could convince people to trust them with. The more they tackled, the more Anah had understood that the only work she could rely on was mercenary and questing, and only with Hailee at her side. No one worried about a fell-touched taking care of some ogres for them, but they didn't want a fell-touched running their store. And Hailee's skillset seemed destined for the same kind of high-risk occupation, her stature forcing clients to take them seriously.

"What does that have to do with taking care of myself?" Anah asked. Her muscles were spasming due to her depleted magic reserves... and her head? The spikes of agony promised a long and painful night.

"You forget to eat. Sometimes you get too busy to wash. You're terrible with people. Plus, you seemed lonely and it was easy to be your friend."

It was Anah's turn to snort. "I'm not an easy friend."

Hailee's grin shone in the candlelight. "Yeah, okay, you aren't. But you're a good one. You and Bucket made adventuring fun for me."

"I thought the fun came from being able to go kicky-kicky at monsters."

"That was just a bonus. Mostly, I liked being paid to spend time with my friends. What we're doing has never mattered that much to me. But you've always seemed to care about the jobs and the money." Hailee grew contemplative. "Yet we kept getting bigger and bigger jobs and earning more and more gold, and now I'm hearing that all along you thought you were weak. What would make you feel capable? What would make you like yourself?"

Anah let the words settle. Hailee wasn't wrong and it was irritating. "I don't know. But I know that I liked you better when you were just an easy-going stomach with fists and none of this introspective feely shit."

But beyond what Hailee had noticed about her, Anah had just heard something new in her friend. Hailee had been doing it for Anah. For friendship. Not once had Hailee expressed that she'd gotten something out of adventuring beyond that.

"Are you happy?" Anah asked.

Hailee tipped her head, her long, black hair spilling down like an inky waterfall. "Most of the time. But the change of the past few days has been nice. Don't you think?"

Anah did think so, but she wasn't ready to admit it aloud. To say something out loud was to make it real. She'd worked for over a decade to try to make herself big enough in power and importance that people didn't immediately dismiss or fear her.

But she'd forgotten to recognize and appreciate the power and importance she already had within.

What if that was like jobs? That she could get more and more of it and never have it be enough?

And if she finally did have enough...what then?

"I'm exhausted," Anah said instead. "Those kids are freaking monsters. We need to find Bucket before we start having an existential crisis, okay?"

Hailee didn't look pleased with the answer, so Anah rolled over and pulled the blanket tight under her chin. The more she and Hailee talked and opened up, the clearer it became that they couldn't return to the way things had been before the temple.

The pain in her head managed to be of some benefit, becoming sharp enough she didn't have room to contemplate anything other than how hurt it was.

ANAH REMAINED IN HER mind throughout the morning. Impulse had brought her to the spice stall in the market. While Snoop and the other children would certainly like toys or sweets as a thank-you, this felt more fitting.

"Mornin'," the gruff merchant said. When he took in her horns, however, his rough demeanor shifted immediately into something more accommodating. Spice dealers were some of the select few who appreciated fell-touched and their desires for intense flavors, and this particular merchant had had dealings with her in the past. "Good to see you again, Miss Anah."

A warm rush accompanied hearing the "Miss" in front of her name, immediately making her think of the children. "Good to see you again, Kip. I've got a list, if you don't mind?"

"I never mind when people wish to spend coin." He punctuated this with a wink, and Anah refrained from shaking her head. Instead, she handed over the parchment she'd scribbled on before leaving the Drunken Goat.

Kip went about his stall, measuring out powders and leaves into small vials and bags. Anah tallied the cost in her head, knowing it was probably more than she should spend. Despite the knowledge, the investment left her buzzing with excitement.

In the end, she handed over two gold coins to cover the wares. It didn't leave her with much leftover. Hailee watched on in curiosity, pulling a face when she heard the total cost.

When they returned to the trek toward the temple, Hailee couldn't contain her need to know any longer, blurting out, "Why in the hells did we just drop all that money on spices? Do you know something I don't?"

Anah smirked. "I know many things you don't. In this case, however, it's for cooking lunches with the children. It'll be easier to endure this ridiculous guise if I'm eating food that actually has flavor. You asked me about taking care of myself. Eating well is a start."

Her attempt at sounding cool and indifferent didn't fool Hailee one bit, but her companion was kind enough not to pursue the topic.

Thankfully, none of the previous day's stench lingered when they entered the temple. There were significantly fewer patrons there to honor Dinna, however, and a twinge of guilt tugged at Anah. A temple as well-maintained as this one required constant support from patrons.

Pearl met them in the classroom, the children scattered and playing. All but one. Anah's brow furrowed. "Where's Snoop?" she asked Pearl.

"He's having some reflection time." Pearl's tone was neutral, but Anah couldn't stop the surge of panic within. It felt as if she were back at her crèche, in trouble once again, and placed in a small room for hours—sometimes days—by herself. The punishment had been emotional agony and, based on how sweaty her palms had grown, had left some scars in her.

"Why? Where? For how long?" Anah spun around as if she'd suddenly see a box with Snoop huddled inside.

Hailee's hand landed on her shoulder and squeezed gently. "Whoa, Anah. What's going on?"

She and Pearl were watching Anah with caution. Filling her lungs with a deep inhalation, Anah waited for her pulse to return to normal. She hadn't noticed she'd been heated until the smell of smoke hit her nose.

"Sorry," she breathed out. "Some bad memories."

Pearl's features shifted with concern. "I'm sorry. He's having reflection time because of his choices leading to yesterday's events. Snoop's in my office. And he's been in there for ten minutes and has another five remaining."

It was... so... reasonable.

"Oh. Right." Sensing that further explanation was warranted, Anah added, "My experience in an orphanage wasn't pleasant."

Pearl softened. "I'm sorry to hear that. Though it makes your talent at this all the more impressive."

Anah choked on a laugh. "Talent? Just yesterday you were dressing me down in the courtyard. Rightfully so, too, as we had allowed it to happen."

The acolyte's cheeks went crimson and her gaze darted back and forth between Hailee and Anah. "That wasn't fair. The entire situation hasn't been fair. You walked through the door, and I just tossed you in there and said to keep them fed and alive. For all intents and purposes, you've done the job I asked you to do."

Hailee held up a hand for a high five. Anah stared at it long enough that her friend pouted before moving it to Pearl, who reluctantly acquiesced. Hailee probably wouldn't wash that hand for a week if her crush was still going strong.

Pearl continued. "No, I'm referring to Snoop's confession. I've never, *never* heard him own up to his mistakes. Certainly not to save someone else's hide. Yet yesterday he did exactly that. He's growing and changing, the two things our goddess most wishes for, and you're the one to thank for that. So thank you."

This left Anah stunned and baffled. These emotional conversations were infinitely more difficult to navigate than making deals with clients. And there'd been so many of them recently that it wasn't just her magical reserve that had been tapped, but also her inner Well of Feeling Things.

"Thank you." It was all she could think of to say.

Pearl nodded before casting one last, long look at Hailee through lowered lashes. If Hailee didn't ask the acolyte out soon, Anah would go nuts over their ridiculous back and forth. After Pear left to get Snoop, Anah shook herself to cast off the lingering feelings within like a dog shaking water off fur.

Hailee rounded them up for morning exercise. Snoop slunk in shortly after, joining the group quietly. He was withdrawn and quiet.

After, with her arms and legs trembling from the exertion, Anah took her place at the front of the room, with everyone else seated in a circle in front.

"We're going to discuss two things as a group this morning."

Hope scooted closer, prompting the others to follow her lead. Anah smiled patiently.

"First, I know yesterday was not our best day." When she caught Snoop's expression starting to fall, she rushed. "But I was so impressed with each of you for joining in the efforts to fix things. Because of that, I've brought a gift."

Happy gasps and wide eyes greeted this announcement. Anah pulled out the bag of wares from the vendor. "I'm going to pass these around. You can smell them first, and we'll use them to cook later, okay?"

Hailee added, "Don't inhale too deeply. Gentle smells, friends."

Anah could imagine Stevie getting an enormous sniff of hot pepper and sneezing the classroom to cinders.

She opened each baggie or vial and explained what it was before passing it around. Cinnamon, coriander, curry leaves, cumin. Hot pepper, truffle salt, lemon salt, mint. As the children smelled each one, Anah relished seeing how their faces morphed and changed. Sometimes there was delight and often wariness, but it was clear they were interested.

"I want you to think of ways you'd like to try these, okay? When we make lunch, you can choose some to use."

The prospect of being the ones to make tasting decisions elated the children, and Anah felt a lightness in her chest that made it easier to breathe.

"Now for the second discussion. How did it go with your parents after yesterday's shenanigans?"

Stump and Bruiser shared a look before shrugging. "Mom didn't care," Stump said while, at the same time, Bruiser squeaked, "Dad thought it was funny."

For once, Cheese didn't appear nonplussed. Her pointed ears drooped and her usually animated tail lay flat on the floor.

"My parents talked about pulling me out last night," she confessed. No one could miss the fear and heartbreak in the cat-girl. "The only reason I wasn't was because it wasn't my fault, they said. But now I'm worried they'll move me to the ornwas-only school, where they're sooooooo stiff and boring. I like my friends here."

Hailee reached over and rubbed Cheese's back. Anah added, "I'm sorry to hear that, Cheese. I bet that was scary and I'm glad you're here."

Cheese's ears perked up and her tail gave a happy flick.

"Stevie, any trouble at your place?" Hailee prompted.

The dragonling held out his hand and tipped it back and forth to say *so-so*.

Hope didn't need to be asked. She burst in. "My moms had a really long fight about it because they were worried that I was with bad influences but then my mom said if one of the students made the bomb they must be really smart and that if you were able to get the smell out you must also be really smart and told my other mom I needed to stay because I needed some of that smart to rub off on me." She paused to take a breath.

"But I don't know how that works because being smart is in your brain and you can't reach your brain to rub any off on me. And that sounds yucky, anyway."

"Your finger's probably scratched your brain at least once," Cheese teased. "With all the nose-picking you do."

The others snickered but Hope only smiled and shook her head. "Nope. I'd know it if I did, I think."

Snoop started to make a joke about Hope's ability to think so Anah cut him off. "Snoop." He flinched, looking at his hands in his lap. "I'm glad you didn't get into too much trouble. I'm interested in why you made the bomb and placed it where it was." Anah's pulse quickened. "Was it because of the things going missing?"

His face jerked up, and he stared at her in awe. "Yes."

Anah managed to keep her face neutral, but the rush of excitement within was substantial. "I'm going to venture that you were trying to catch someone," she carefully said.

"How did you know?" Snoop asked while Hailee looked up sharply, understanding where Anah was going with her inquiry.

"I know because Miss Hailee and I have also been trying to find the thief. And I think we should pool our resources and work together."

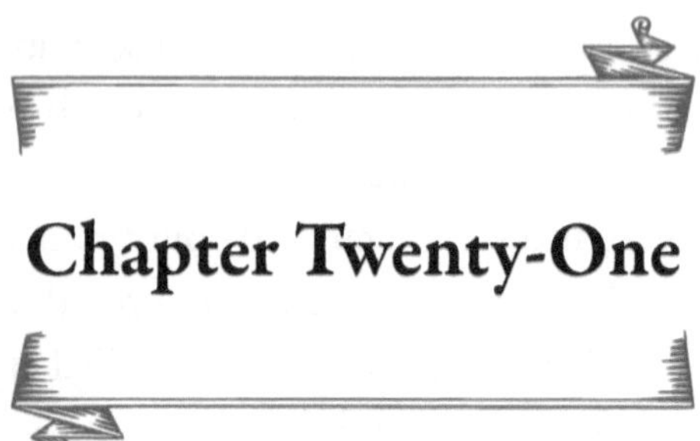

# Chapter Twenty-One

The slate was erased and was propped up, ready for use. Anah held a piece of chalk and the kids looked on, eager to participate in the new lesson.

"Okay, here is where we combine what we know." She wrote a word on the board—kids—then she drew a line under it. "Snoop. I'd like you to tell me who exactly the stink bomb was for."

Snoop scratched the side of his head and said "Wells, I think there's someone livin' in the walls. The day Miss Hailee caught me and Cheese in the kitchen, well, we saw some footprints and we noticed a trail leading into one of the vents." He smiled large and bright. "So, I thought I'd set a trap for whoever it is."

Anah tipped her head in recognition of his insights. "I can tell you that I know for certain that there is someone hiding in the walls." The children gasped in awe, as if she had the same scrying power that Miss Pearl had. "Hailee and I have been looking for them as well." She pointed to Hailee. "Would you describe the suspect?"

Hailee, able to roll with whatever came at her, said, "We're dealing with a halfling. They're going to be short. Your height." She pointed to Stump and Bruiser, who were tall for children but right at adult halfling size. "He's known for his ability to hide, to put on excellent disguises, and to nick just about anything off anyone without getting caught."

Cheese leaned forward, her tail making large swoops of interest behind her. "How do you know all this?"

It did not feel as if there were much point in hiding who they were anymore. Or at least, Anah decided, she could give half of the truth to the children. "We've been tracking him. He took something from us, and we want it back."

"What did he take from you?" Snoop had his arms crossed as if he could not decide whether he liked what was happening or not. Anah would need to tread carefully. Snoop was quick to pick up on things and he mistrusted just as quickly.

"He took some loot from us, as well as a valuable wand. The Wand of Birramos, to be specific. It's a fell-magic wand." It was strange how the more she talked about the wand the less important it seemed to be to her. Before the temple, it had been Anah's greatest desire. Now, she found herself struggling to remember that it was why they'd come to the temple in the first place.

"He's taken some of our stuff too!" Hope was rocking back and forth, looking at Anah with bright, shining eyes. "Like he stole my blankie." She sniffled, her nose for once stuffed due to tears.

"And the twins each lost a shoe, and the book." As Snoop listed, he looked everywhere but in Anah's direction. She carefully peered at him, a sinking sensation gathering within.

"What do you mean *the book*?" Now Snoop looked like someone who would be truly happy if the ground split open at that moment and swallowed him whole.

"The book I was allowed to borrow from the temple library," he admitted. Shame dripped from every word, and any anger that Anah might have felt dissipated immediately. It wasn't Snoop's fault that Bucket was taking a wide variety of things. No one could have predicted that the halfling would be stealing from children to begin with. But her frustration lay entirely with Bucket, not the poor little gnome who sat, agitated and upset.

"And now you're worried?" Anah guessed.

Snoop nodded.

"Snoop, I don't want you to feel badly about that. It wasn't your fault."

"I know that it's not my fault," Snoop said slowly. "But I'm afraid that Miss Pearl won't let us take more books out because I lost something so valuable."

"You didn't lose it at all. Someone took it from you, and I'll have you know that Miss Pearl has been aware of things going missing all over the temple." Anah tried to offer a reassuring smile. "So, you don't need to worry, because she will understand that you did not lose it or harm it on purpose or even out of carelessness. Okay?"

He nodded half-heartedly, and Anah hoped that he believed her. She wished she'd had someone say something similar to her all those years ago. Gods, what would have changed in her had she heard even once that something wasn't her fault?

"Is there anything else that you know for certain?"

Snoop rebounded. "Your thief is really messy." He pointed to the vent. "We cleaned all this up yesterday with your magic, but before the bomb went off I discovered a trail of something sticky." He looked mildly devious in a way that probably should have alarmed Anah, but she found herself wanting to laugh instead. Whatever he'd figured out, he was quite proud of himself.

"It was the missing pudding." This was whispered in a conspiratorial way. Even Hailee managed to look shocked.

"The pudding?"

"Yeah. The pudding you thought I ate."

Anah and Hailee shared a look. "I'm not sure I follow," Anah admitted.

Snoop sighed heavily as if he were the one speaking to children. "That first day," he insisted. "Cheese and I were tryin' to take some pudding but you said it was all gone." He shrugged. "I meant it when I said I didn't eat it."

Several things clicked into place for Anah. "So, you think that our thief stole the pudding." She tried to imagine Bucket loading an entire pot full of pudding into the vents and then placing the emptied pot back onto the stove. Where would he have kept the gelatinous dessert? How would he have moved it through the vents?

"So, I've been finding the goopy pudding in our cubbies.' Snoop got up and went over to where his cubby was. He reached into the depths of it, and when he pulled out his hand Anah saw glistening on the tips of his fingers what was clearly old pudding.

"That's very strange." Anah had thought she'd known Bucket before he had left, but she did feel confident that he was not the kind of person to leave sticky messes wherever he went. The halfling was as neat and tidy as he was sneaky . . . and he was very sneaky.

"Okay," she said, knowing that she wasn't going to figure out the pudding situation right away. She made a new word and line on the slate—teachers. "We know"—she gestured between Hailee and herself before continuing to write—"that it's a halfling who is good at sneaking around. And we know he cannot leave the temple."

This caught Cheese's interest. "How do you know he can't leave the temple?" she asked. "Because I'm very sneaky and I know all sorts of ways out."

Anah decided not to think too long or hard on that for the moment, or she would wonder how much trouble these children had gotten into before she'd arrived.

"Because I cast a spell to make sure that he could not leave without my permission." She tapped at her chin thoughtfully. The variety of the things being taken and the addition of the pudding offset any assurance she'd had that Bucket would eventually tire of hiding. Whatever he was doing, he was ramping up his efforts.

"So now we need to decide how we're going to tackle our thief problem." She drew a line and made a new column—ideas.

"Should we tell Miss Pearl?" Hope asked.

"No!" Snoop said vehemently. "She has enough trouble already."

Hailee contributed, "Normally I would encourage all of you to tell an adult when something is strange or doesn't make sense, but"—she gave each of the children a steady look—"you have two adults in the classroom right now. I think Snoop is right, that this isn't something Miss Pearl could help with."

Snoop stuck his tongue out.

"But she has that magic," Cheese insisted. "The one where she can spy on everybody. It's really creepy when she does that."

Anah offered Cheese a look of approval. The ornwas might be lactose intolerant, but she was quick on her feet. "That's good thinking, Cheese. But I already thought of that and it wouldn't work. Miss Pearl has to know where to look and who she's looking for when she scries. She doesn't know the halfling and none of us have any idea where in the temple he's hiding."

"So do we go into the vents?" Snoop asked.

Stevie and the twins tensed with alarm. Anah could already picture what they were imagining. The twins with their larger size getting stuck inside one of the vent corners or tighter nooks. Or Stevie sneezing in close quarters, sending flames to char anyone who was climbing around near them. *No, thank you.*

"I don't think that's what we should pursue either," Anah said gently. "While I appreciate that idea, with the unknowns of the venting and tunnel system as well as several other factors." She sent a wink at the twins and Stevie. "We might do more harm than good."

"We could set a trap," Stump said, wringing the bottom of his shirt. The fabric looked in danger of ripping. Everyone stared at the orc twin. Stump and Bruiser were often silent and more often sweet. It was unexpected that one of them not only had an idea for this situation, but a good idea.

"I like that," Anah said, thinking already of all the different ways that Bucket might be caught. "It will be tough because this halfling is not only very sneaky, he is also quite clever. So, we'll need to come up with something he can't resist." Anah knew Bucket already had quite the trove of jewels and gold. What else would tempt him?

"That's easy," Snoop said with the confidence of a large, grown man, rather than a small gnome who'd been overlooked and misjudged for the entirety of his short life. *Good for you, Snoop.* "Most of what he's been taking has been stuff you'd need to survive, right?" He rubbed at his belly. "And if he's been living on only pudding, I bet he's ready for something new. After all, I love pudding, but I don't think I could eat it every meal every day without getting sick of it."

Cheese stretched and purred. "Mmmm, I could," she said, licking at her lips and whiskers. "Especially if the pudding was made with heavy cream."

Hope immediately appeared panicked, and Anah could understand why. Cheese's gastrointestinal system was quick to react to dairy in violently toxic ways.

"That's brilliant," Hailee said, giving Snoop a high five. "Bucket always did like the finer things in life. He just didn't like doing honest work to get them."

That had always been part of the fun. How she, Bucket, and Hailee would finagle their way into upper-class spaces they had no business in, just so the halfling could eat rare and exotic foods or brush elbows with nobles and dignitaries.

"How do you know that he doesn't like to do honest work?" Snoop asked. The curiosity skating over his features made Anah's stomach sour. She'd always appreciated it when people around her were able to keep up, but Snoop was seeing and understanding too much. While she'd admitted that they knew there was a halfling in the temple, she hadn't hinted about how they knew him or what all of them were doing in Dinna's house. She was worried that if Snoop believed he would be abandoned again, he may not help at all, but turn them into Pearl, who might call city officials.

In past experience, city constables were eager to pin crimes on people they didn't like, and very few liked infernal cambions. Anah wasn't sure if impersonating teachers was illegal per se, but she was one-hundred-percent sure it was not well looked upon. Therefore, she'd rather not deal with the outcome that would inevitably explode from being discovered.

"I'm hungry." Anah wasn't, but food was the easiest distraction she could come up with. "We should work on lunch and while we do, we can try out different dishes that we might be able to entice the halfling with."

The children lit up at the reminder of the spices.

"We can turn it into an experiment," Anah added, stoking the fires of their interest. "Posit what spices would go well with what foods, then make them, taste them, and write down whether our assumptions were right or wrong."

No one was even looking at the slate. They were clamoring to line up at the door. Her diversion worked. Snoop's face was one of someone already scheming and planning. Anah had to trust it was aimed at Bucket and not at Hailee and her.

"We can set a trap with the food, like Stump suggested." She smiled at the entire class. "And once we've trapped him and retrieved our things, we can figure out how to handle such a cheeky little thief."

Delight rippled through tiny bodies. They were being trusted with a big-person problem. Their whispers were a flurry of ideas, some outlandish and many downright messed up. But one thing was for sure; they were proud to be a part of the mission, which was now their sole focus.

What she didn't want to say, or even think about, was what would happen for all of them—she, Hailee, Bucket, and Miss Pearl and the kids—if they succeeded.

# Chapter Twenty-Two

While Hailee and most of the children cleaned up from an interesting but mostly tasty lunch, Snoop sidled up to Anah and sat quietly beside her. "Miss Anah?" he asked, looking at his shoes rather than at her. "Will the food really work?"

Anah mulled it over. "Well, we know that he's very clever, and he's very sneaky. So we can't trick him in any sort of obvious way." They were sitting on top of the table so that their legs dangled. She kicked her feet back and forth as she thought. The plan as it was relied on Bucket getting desperate. But while he preferred things easy and upper-class, he also liked not being caught.

"I wish that I wasn't so tapped with my magic, because then I could make a binding circle," she mused.

"A binding circle?"

"Yeah," she explained. "A binding circle is a way of snaring unsuspecting people with magic. The size of the circle makes a difference for how much magic is expended. And while the thief may be small, I think he'll be too wary of approaching the food head on." She imagined how she could fit a circle inside an entire room, spreading it so that there was no spot for Bucket to put his tiny, stealing feet without being trapped by her magic. It was a pleasurable fantasy. Anah pictured his face screwing up in fear as soon as he realized the mistake he'd made. Well, one of many mistakes he'd made. The first of which had been stealing from Anah in the first place and deserting her.

It still rankled her that he hadn't felt he could just come to her with any concerns. Yes, she could be blunt, but she'd thought they'd learned to read each other well. Bucket had been quick to make her laugh and sympathetic when she raged.

"And you don't have the magic to make that happen?" Snoop sounded more like he was thinking rather than judging her, so Anah simply shrugged in agreement. It was the kind of vulnerability that usually unleashed her deepest insecurities, but it was also a fact. He reached into his pocket and held something in his hands. They were gripped tight so she couldn't see within.

"I want to give you something," he said nervously. "But I don't want to get in any trouble for it."

Anah tilted her head, curious. When was the last time she'd received a gift from anyone? When you were an adventurer, there wasn't much room for presents. You pretty much just took what you wanted. "I promise I won't be upset." She knew she would have to keep that promise regardless of what he held in his hands, because she had experienced people breaking those sorts of promises herself. It was not a good feeling or beneficial toward building trust.

"So like Cheese was sayin'. The vents are sort of like a maze system. And she and I have mapped out quite a bit of it." he admitted. "It gets kinda boring sometimes. Well, I mean before you and Miss Hailee showed up it was boring sometimes, now we have exciting stuff every day." He looked up at her with wide-eyed enthusiasm. And Anah found herself chuckling out loud, not sure if Snoop understood he was at the root of much of the excitement. "So I used the vents last night after everyone went to sleep."

Now Anah was very interested. Not only in hearing that Snoop and Cheese had regularly used the vents to get around—that didn't surprise her in the least—but that he'd used it right on the heels of being in such deep trouble with Pearl. Whatever he'd wanted, he'd wanted it bad. "So, you were doing a little late-night sneaking yourself?" She raised her eyebrows conspiratorially.

Snoop Dug turned a brilliant shade of pink. "I know I wasn't supposed to, but I needed to get something for you as an apology. You got yelled at for somethin' that was my fault. And you almost had to leave. You were willing to let it happen just to keep me out of trouble." His hands rolled around with the item inside, nervous and jittery. "It meant a lot to me. I never had anyone that wasn't a kid go out on a limb for me before. And I feel like it means more coming from you."

"And why is that, Snoop?" Anah resisted the urge to reach out and put a hand on his shoulder, but she was surprised at how natural and heartwarming the conversation was between the little gnome and herself. She also wasn't sure what it said about her that she felt closer and more at ease with a mischievous child than she did with most adults. Best not to dwell on it.

"Wells, I just wanted to say thank you. So I snuck out and I found something I thought you'd like." He opened his tiny hand and inside rested a clear vial that was filled with a pale, glowing liquid. Anah knew what it was in an instant, and it took her breath away.

"Where did you get that?" she murmured, awe laced in every word.

"I know stealin's wrong, but I don't have any money. So I took it from a stall that's just outside the temple. I didn't get caught, I swear."

Snoop was holding a miniscule vial of fell water. The amount didn't matter. Just a few drops would help restore her natural magic balance. A vial of that size would bring her to almost half-potency. Between the vial and a week's worth of rest, she'd be at full power. But Anah didn't have a week, she didn't think. Bucket wasn't even trying to be inconspicuous. All the things he was taking were being noticed and cataloged. It wouldn't be long before the temple fought to bring in someone a lot like her to root him out.

"This is a very nice gift," she said softly, holding her hand open. He dropped the vial in it, and she felt the tightness in her chest begin to release. It was a cinched sensation she hadn't even known was there until it left. "I'd rather you not sneak out of the temple because there isn't anyone to keep you out of trouble," Anah replied. She couldn't stop looking at the small vial, which suddenly felt priceless. "But, this gift means so much to me. And it will help in our quest to catch our thief. Thank you."

Snoop just kicked his feet harder, then launched himself off the table to run and help wash dishes with Cheese and the twins. His assistance would most likely cause the washing to devolve into a suds fight.

Anah was left sitting with a vial of an incredibly precious substance in her hands. Fell water had to be blessed by a demon, which was a bit of an oxymoron in and of itself. Finding a demon who was willing to put his blessing on water was difficult enough, but usually those same demons required a payment in return that few people were willing to give. Therefore, a vial of this size would cost at minimum a platinum piece. Something that most people didn't just have hanging around in their coin purses and why she didn't carry around a stock of it.

Anah eyed the prize, knowing that to accept it was to put herself in debt to Snoop Dug. Yes, it was an apology gift, but it was also a princely gift. She felt she couldn't just take the gift and walk away with ease, not like she used to. Anah decided she couldn't make any hard choices until she'd restored some of her magic and finished this business with Bucket. She uncorked the vial and swallowed the fell water in one go.

The surge of power within her veins crackled and raced. It was the most delicious kind of burn. The heat of the hells meeting with her body on a cellular level. Bringing her demonic heritage to the forefront. She missed this feeling. And while she did not appreciate its evil roots and the way those roots hounded her every step, she did love the feeling of riotous power.

Anah wiggled her fingers, relishing the magic within them. With this, she could cast a binding spell that would cover an entire room. Nothing that touched it would be able to be free without her permission.

By the end of this she'd have the wand and answers. Anah just hoped there was enough time to prepare herself to hear why Bucket snuck off and deserted them.

THE CLASSROOM WAS VETOED as a potential spot for the trap. For one, it was the only classroom in the temple and the children were fearful of more of their stuff being taken. Also, Hailee might inadvertently wreck some of the furniture if it came to a wrestling contest. There'd been a time in Anah's youth when she'd gone to a traveling carnival and watched as grown men tried to catch a piglet that had been covered in linseed oil. They would wrap their massive arms around the tiny porcine creature, only for it to wriggle free and tear across the mud, evading even the fastest and most deft participants. She could easily see that same situation with Bucket managing to duck, evade, and twist out of Hailee's strong arms and fast advances, making for a chase that would take up every square inch of room in the class and leave shattered everything in its path.

Cheese had been the one to suggest using the pantry that was nearby. It wasn't the pantry for the kitchen proper, but rather the larder where the temple stored their long-term food stuffs. There was preserved water and fruits inside. Pots of fermented vegetables lined shelves and large bags of flour heaped along one side of the wall. Anah could smell a magical enchantment surrounding the flour, shielding it from rodents. It was a cozy and comfortable setup. But more importantly, it was about as large a space as she had the power to fully and securely bind.

Anah went to work. Sweat beaded on her brow as she murmured in infernal and used a sliver of charcoal from the kitchen hearth to mark spaces where the spell would take hold. Behind her was an audience, Hailee and the kids peeking through, their faces rapt with interest.

The spellcasting took her more time than she'd anticipated and almost all of the magic that the fell water had given back to her to finish. Anah had devoted more to it then she would normally, knowing there wouldn't be a second chance.

Anah stood and brushed the smudged charcoal from her hands. "All right. The binding spell is done. Snoop, Cheese, where are the vents in here?" Snoop started to enter but Hailee grabbed his collar, stopping him from taking a step inside. Anah held up her hands to signal they should stay back.

"You can't actually come in here now. The next person who puts their feet inside will get trapped in the circle. It will catch anybody or anything. Not just the thief." If Anah had managed to hold on to some of Bucket's hair or an item of his, she might have been able to attune it to just the halfling, much like the spell containing him in the temple. As it was, she had to make a generalized spell more thorough and complex so that no one—not even a rogue as sneaky as Bucket—could outsmart it.

Snoop stared down in wonder before pointing to the two spots where the vents connected into the larder. They were high up, but she could see how someone small and light on their feet would be able to sneak down. She made sure that her magic pulsed at the very base of them and all the way down. The finishing touch was the bait, a picnic basket with an array of foods within. Fresh warm bread with coriander and garlic baked into it. There was also a stew of mutton with raisins and cinnamon and cumin, and, thanks to Stump, an overly healthy dose of hot peppers. The children had decided that it was too much heat for them, but Anah had found it perfect and was sad to see the rest of it left out for her treacherous former friend.

She arranged the food to make it look as though someone had been packing a picnic and had to rush off at the last minute. Then, using a smidge of fire, she coaxed the air into enough movement to send the smells and steam of the food into the vents. The trap was set.

It was then—not earlier, when it would have been useful—that Hailee pointed out the obvious. "How are we going to know when he is caught?"

Anah wrinkled her nose in frustration. There was only a single entrance and exit to the larder. It wasn't exactly a space meant for high occupancy. Yet if they stood in the hall and waited there was no way Bucket wouldn't notice their presence. And if they were found, he wouldn't take the bait.

"I think I have a solution." She reached in the pocket of her skirt and pulled out the vial. It was empty save for a few drops. Anah, with as much dignity as she could muster, tipped the vial over and shook and sucked the rest out. The rush was nowhere near as potent or pleasurable as the first sips had been, but there was enough now for her to do a single final enchantment. She went and touched each of the children and Hailee, pressing into them immunity to her charmed circle. It was honestly too much magic to be spending, and by the end of it, her head was throbbing. Thinking became a chore.

"There," she breathed, sounding raspier than was healthy. "Find some hiding spaces. I think that I've been able to make sure none of you will get stuck and your presence in the room should be hidden for the most part, assuming you're not in plain sight or banging giant pots and pans."

The children took their orders seriously, quickly murmuring and chattering amongst themselves as they discussed the best places to hide. Anah resisted the urge to slap a palm against her forehead. They were going to give up the trap before it had even sprung from sheer noisiness. But to her surprise, the children just as quickly found places to hide and, in less time than she would have believed, all of them were hidden. Had she just walked into the larder without any knowledge, Anah would be hard-pressed to know that there were six children hidden amongst the goods. It was very impressive, the kind of stealth that Bucket had brought to the table.

Hailee, on the other hand, was a flippin' giant compared to the rest of them. A giant in a tiny room.

Hailee shrugged. "I don't think I can do that." She looked around a bit more and then shook her head. "Nope. Definitely can't do that."

Anah sighed. "Let me give you a sending stone." She gave her a tiny rock that they'd both used frequently in past adventures to communicate with each other over short distances. Hailee nodded, taking her rock and skipping out the door. She would hide somewhere close by, and would come running as soon as Anah used her stone.

Anah managed to slip herself between two shelves, using a bit of the food's protective cloth to mask her presence. Now they would wait. She prayed it wouldn't be a long wait, because the children were already being asked to do quite a bit, and she could just imagine Hope struggling with a full bladder.

It was remarkably quiet in the larder, and the smells of the food threatened to make her tummy grumble despite having just eaten a large and filling lunch. "Okay, everyone. We have to be silent," she said. Though it was as much for herself as it was for the children. When she didn't hear a response, she could picture Snoop rolling his eyes and Cheese flashing him a "can you believe this woman?" face.

Time ticked by and she began to see the flaws in their operation. In the past, she'd been quick to think of plans, Hailee ready to implement them, and—as Anah could painfully see—Bucket to poke holes in it. Each of them had a job and without one it all wobbled precariously.

Bucket would have known children shouldn't be included in a waiting game. Those were difficult enough for adults. He would have foreseen needing to attune them to her spell before and not after. There were likely ten or twelve other mistakes she couldn't see, and the stabbing headache erased any chance of Anah figuring them out.

She wasn't in so much pain, however, to miss the itsy, bitsy thought that popped up, unwanted and intrusive. That perhaps she was keeping her magic reserves low on purpose.

That maybe she'd rushed into the trap without considering all the ways it might go awry with the hopes it would fail. If it failed, they'd have to stay. Hailee and Miss Pearl would get more time together, Anah would be able to introduce the children to more flavors and stories, and Bucket . . . well, being trapped in Dinna's space with no place at the table might be punishment enough.

Oh.

*Oh.*

Anah wished she could move, if only to escape her runaway thoughts. Because it couldn't be that, right? She didn't actually enjoy this job. That was ridiculous. Kids were gross and silly and they needed things, just all the time with the needing and demanding and challenging and—

And yet.

Something cut through her panicked personal crisis like a sword through, well, pudding. A rustle.

Anah held her breath, heart racing like a rabbit.

It came again.

The rustle became a scurry, the clamoring sound of something in the vents unmistakable.

The trap had *worked.*

# Chapter Twenty-Three

What happened next happened quickly. Bucket burst from a vent and fell to the floor, immediately trapped by Anah's magic. His face was contorted with panic. He wasn't in good shape. His clothing was filthy. He didn't look particularly well fed. Certainly not like someone who had been munching on pudding for multiple days. This was not the put-together and confident Bucket she knew.

Anah stood and moved from her hiding place.

"Hello, Bucket." She struggled to remain calm but she could feel the fire underneath her skin, eager to flare to life as soon as she lost control of the reins on her emotions. "It's good to see you again."

Perhaps what startled her the most was that Bucket's look of fear didn't intensify when she spoke to him. In fact, when Bucket saw Anah, he almost looked relieved, if only for the flicker of a second. "Oh, Anah!"

He tried to stand.

Then Bucket floundered as he strained against the binding circle. The spell was some of her best work, all things considered. Anah had put every bit of her magic and intensity into it, ensuring that it was masterfully done, and not likely to screw up. Bucket struggled despite the futility. "Anah, we've got to go now."

She didn't move. She was a rock that he wouldn't be able to trick or hurt again. "Why would we need to do that? I've got you exactly where I want you." She grasped the sending stone and held it to her mouth. "Hailee, we've got the little bugger."

This snagged some of Bucket's interest. "Is Hailee here? Good! We're going to need her. But first, can you please unstick me?"

There wasn't time to consider this as the children emerged from their hiding spots from all over the larder, whooping with triumph. Snoop marched right up to Bucket and seemed thoroughly pleased by the fact that he was almost the same height as the halfling. He poked Bucket in the chest. "You's the one who's been stealin' our pudding."

Bucket barked out a surprised and awful laugh. "Stealing your pudding? Oh no. The pudding has been stealing from *me*."

This took time to process. Anah's mind kept running the sentence over and over, trying to see if there was actual meaning in the nonsense. "What do you mean the pudding has been stealing from you?"

Bucket pressed his hands together in a pleading gesture. "Anah, I swear that I will tell you everything, but we have to get out of here now."

There had been several escapades with Bucket and Hailee in the past where Bucket's ability to act like he was in shambles had been the very thing that had helped him elude being caught. She was not about to believe him now. Hailee was on her way and they were going to use the tight space of the larder to make sure the little bastard wouldn't give them the slip this time.

Bucket strained, twisting his body as much as he could with parts that weren't bound by the magic, looking with expectant horror over his shoulder at the vent. Anah couldn't help it. She lifted her gaze and peered closely, wondering what exactly he thought was about to happen. When nothing did, she dropped her stare back to him, pinning him with it just as much as her magic held him rooted. "You've been very busy these past few days."

Bucket looked as if he might begin to weep. Anah had never seen him cry. They weren't exactly a gang of crying friends, so this was something she couldn't interpret. Was it desperation to escape? Or was it possible that Bucket truly was afraid of something?

Before she could figure it out though, there was a loud squelching sound. Between the door and the hallway, a large mass had dropped from just outside. It was roughly the size of a small pony, though there was no discernable shape. The surface was yellow and cream-colored, though the colors shifted, moved, and swirled. There were no eyes she could see, but she had an awful sensation that it was intently watching her. It moved. It wobbled. It vibrated.

It smelled cloyingly sweet and like vanilla.

Anah pointed at it. "Did you seriously mean pudding?" Her voice carried a hysterical edge.

Bucket wailed, fully hysterical. "Oh no! It's too late!"

The mound of pudding gave a little shimmy.

Anah was usually much more responsive in situations with immediate danger, but she had never been in a situation with an enormous, possibly sentient mass of pudding. What exactly was the protocol here? Did they attack it with spoons?

What really mattered, she understood with horror, was that she was trapped with the children. They were stuck inside because of her. She couldn't care less about Bucket being in harm's way, but the children were an entirely different matter. They didn't have experience fighting any sort of monster. They had no weapons and no plan. And each and every one of them was shaking with terror, staring at the thing that undulated with menace.

She needed to get the children to safety immediately. But *how*?

Though muffled, Hailee's voice traveled through the pudding. "What in the hells is this?"

"I think it's the missing pudding!" Anah shouted back, feeling ridiculous. It was... a lot to take in. But while she processed she pointed to Snoop, getting his attention. She mouthed, "You have to run" and pointed to the vent Bucket had sprang from. At first Snoop seemed to shake his head like he wouldn't leave, but then the pudding took a little globulous slurp toward them. Anah wasn't exactly sure what it could do to them, but Bucket's fear was a measure of how seriously she needed to take it.

She pointed at the vent with more insistence, and Snoop reconsidered his decision to try and stay. He grabbed Cheese, and together they hustled the other children over to the vent. It was up high on the wall, not within easy reach of them. The twins worked first, hoisting Hope up into the vent. She crawled in. Next went Cheese, only Cheese was reluctant to get into the vent. She kept looking back at Anah and making a nod as if the teacher could follow them. Anah would, but she had to make sure they were out of the way first.

"I think I'm going to try to punch it," came Hailee's voice.

Before Anah could say "You can't punch pudding, dumbass" she saw the entirety of the pudding ripple and shake like water did when something hit the ground nearby. There was a *sluuuurrrp*-like sucking noise, and Anah couldn't help the fear burning in her chest. She pictured her friend being pulled into the blob's center and suffocating.

"Hailee, are you okay?" Anah cried out.

For a moment, there were only the sounds of wet smacking and slurping and general squelching. It was enough to make her nauseous, but then, thankfully, Hailee said, "Yeah, I'm okay, but I don't think I can kick its butt."

Anah refrained from pointing out that even the tiniest bit of common sense could have let Hailee know that amorphous sludge beings didn't have butts to kick. The pudding creature didn't have a mouth either, or any sort of discernible feature to let Anah know what it was thinking, but it did have a sort of pissed-off vibe now radiating out that she truly did not like. It slid another inch into the larder, making the atmosphere suddenly and intensely claustrophobic. Anah looked at the vent again and knew for certain that there was no way all of the children would be able to get out before the pudding came in.

"Bucket! How do we fight this thing?"

Bucket stared at her incredulously. "You don't fight it! It's a freaking dessert! You run from it! I was running from it until your stupid magic spell caught me. Now let me go!"

Anah found herself embarrassed under all the terror. She'd poured everything into the spell. Now the well was too dry to release him.

As horrible a consideration as it was, she could leave Bucket. Use him as bait for the pudding. It could do… whatever it was it did to him while she made sure the kids got out safely. She should do that, right? Bucket was the little thief who had brought them to this moment in the first place. She had been ready to absolutely torture the snot out of the little bugger. But now that he was in front of her, trembling and looking rather awful, she found that there was more than an ounce of sympathy telling her she couldn't leave him. This was her friend of so many years. Thievery and deception or not, she wasn't ready to sacrifice him to whatever devious dessert gods were out there.

Snoop turned around. "Can you hits it with a spell? Maybe some fire? You could torch it!"

That wasn't a terrible idea. Anah's head was absolutely pounding, but the panic and adrenaline of the moment were keeping her present. She reached deep within her, trying to find every last thread of anger, of frustration, of all the things that helped her infernal blood light itself afire. She managed a few tiny flames licking along her skin. Even this, her most basic strength, had been overtaxed.

It would have to be enough. She stepped cautiously toward the pudding, wary of its every wobble and bubble. Breath hitching, she placed her flaming hand against its awful, gelatinous surface.

Anah's stomach roiled and threatened to spew. The sensation of the viscous, chilled surface against her flaming palm was just about the most disgusting experience she'd ever had. The texture made her skin crawl, and her spine felt as if it were going to leap out of her body and run away, just so her nervous system wouldn't have to experience this tactile sensation ever again. But the pudding withdrew. It seemed to be sort of whimpering? She couldn't describe how she had heard it, only that it did *not* like the heat. She tried to pull up more flames, encouraged by the way the pudding shied away from her. But unfortunately...

She was absolutely, positively, one hundred percent out of magic. There wasn't a drop. There wasn't a dribble. There was nothing in her for even her most basic powers. Her infernal blood had well and truly failed her.

Anah scrambled back when the pudding glopped out a tendril at her. She could picture it sucking in her hand, trapping her. Her brain cultivated the feel of that awful, awful substance touching every inch of her skin and she was fairly certain that she would die from being absolutely squicked out long before the oxygen disappeared.

Snoop came to her side, grabbing her hand. He tugged her back. Hailee yelled through the blob once more. "Anah! I'm going to try to piss it off. Maybe it will chase me and you and the kids can escape."

A rush of relief pounded through Anah. She didn't think she could handle any more of the pudding. And it did seem to have emotions, because it responded in grotesque rippling waves that communicated its displeasure and, she thought understood now, its hunger.

Over the top of it, Anah barely made out movement as Hailee heaved a chair at the mass.

There was a *thwapppppp,* and the pudding shook again heavily. She waited for it to start to inch out of the larder, but it didn't. It maintained its steadfast hold, right in the middle of the doorway that was the only entrance and exit into the larder, apart from the vent Anah wasn't certain that she could even fit in.

The legs of the chair rotated around in the gloopy surface before being slowly sucked in. It was a promise. Worse, Anah saw the pudding blob *grow.* All the stolen items had been its appetizers, allowing it to grow to a size where it was primed to hunt down the main dishes.

Them.

Bucket, anguished, cried out once more. "Anah! For the love of all the gods. Please!"

Anah looked at him in total, honest sympathy. She had to accept she wasn't enough. Her magic wasn't powerful or great enough to make up for her size, her heritage, her inability to believe in herself. The words slipped from her mouth. "I can't."

He whimpered. Bucket's large eyes watered and the tears spilled over. "You can't leave me here, Anah. Whatever you think I've done, you can't leave me here."

"You don't understand!" Her voice cracked, shame crawling into the words. "I actually can't. I'm out of magic. I can't even catch on fire."

The seriousness of the situation ruined Anah. She was the in-charge adult in the room. She had no magic. She had a disheveled halfling stuck to the floor. And she had six trembling, shaking children who had been entrusted to her care and who'd shown her kindness and respect. They saw her as someone to look up to, not someone to kick when she was down.

In her quest for the wand that should've made her immune to failing, Anah had royally screwed the pooch.

# Chapter Twenty-Four



Death by pudding had to be the dumbest way to go. Pearl would be unable to explain it to the parents because Anah couldn't even explain how the sugary, devouring mass had come to be. Hailee might be smart enough to run and survive, but Anah doubted it. Her friend's loyalty would lead her right into the goopy pits of this hellish creature.

More *thwips* and *thwops* sounded as Hailee threw things into it, yelling to get its attention.

The pudding continued to grow, now taking up the majority of the doorway.

"Hailee, you have to stop!" Anah screamed.

She heard a sort of frustrated grunt, followed by a stomach-curdling squeak, before there was a huge *wubbbblublublubblubblub*. "That'll get its attention!" Hailee sounded triumphant. "I just threw an entire desk into it!"

Ice ran through Anah's normally fiery veins as the pudding almost doubled in size. The sides of it stretched and grew rectangular, a distorted mimicry of the furniture it had just been fed.

Had it been any normal creature, it might have stuck fast in the doorway at that size, halting its progression. But the pudding had an advantage, and that was no solidity. It continued to wobble and move and stretch as it slid into the larder. Instead of slurping a tiny bit forward, it shimmied itself in until Bucket was mere inches away from its gooey surface.

There was nothing she could do. Anah sank to her knees, despair zapping her strength. She selfishly knew she'd throw herself at it first because she was too much a coward to watch the children be consumed.

But then, something in the atmosphere shifted. A strength bubbled up, not in the pudding, but in the gnome beside her.

Snoop took charge. He gave her a reassuring pat between the horns. It was utterly ridiculous that, in this situation with death oozing towards them, she received such reassurance from somebody so small and so young. She was the one who was supposed to be making him feel better. Yet his easy touch and comforting petting calmed her system down enough to reassess. She broke the news to him.

"I think I'm out of ideas."

He nodded slowly, and at first she assumed he was bravely facing down their inevitable absorption. But then... there was a twist to his features that reminded her of gears smoothly turning and she saw it—the moment an idea popped into his clever little noggin.

"I've got it." Then, bracingly, his shy reserve came back. "If it's ok? It might be... messy."

She couldn't have stopped the startled and desperate giggle that escaped her even if she'd wanted to. He was afraid of getting in trouble even at this moment? "Snoop, if you get us out of this, you can make the biggest mess you've ever made and I will love you just as much as I do now."

Snoop paled and froze. But he rallied and rushed back over to his classmates. Hope remained the only child in the vent. She peered down, apparently nonplussed by the situation, a finger probing a nostril. Snoop stared at her before, with a visible shudder, he said, "Hope, I needs some of your boogers."

Hope was delighted by this request, happily managing to scrape several very large, golden nuggets out of her nostrils. She passed them down to Snoop, who was turning green around the tips of his gray-skinned face as he collected them. Soon, he had enough to roll into a tacky ball. He went over to some larder shelves. Snoop scanned until he found what he was looking for—a can of cooking oil.

Moving quickly, Snoop stripped off his shirt and doused it in oil. Over this, he stretched his booger ball until it formed a sticky shell. Anah could see how tacky it was by the way it clung to his fingers. She wasn't sure what Snoop was up to, but Anah was certain if she survived she would be haunted by nightmares of this plan.

Snoop handed the awful device to Bruiser, who was reluctant to take it. "I need you to throw this at the pudding." Bruiser didn't hesitate, most likely not wanting to have Hope's boogers in his hands for longer than necessary. He heaved, and as sweet as that boy was, he had an arm on him. The booger ball sliced through the air, whapping onto the surface of the pudding. Anah could see it starting to pull it in, but fifty percent of the ball still remained exposed to the surface.

Snoop paled. "I didn't mean just yet!"

"Sorry." Bruiser didn't sound sorry.

Frantic, Snoop turned to Cheese. "I need you to fart."

Cheese opened her mouth as if to say something, shut it, opened it again. "But I've been good! I haven't had any dairy!"

For a second Snoop lost his confidence, his great plan foiled by a lactose-free obstacle. But then he took a deep breath and did something so horrifically brave and awful that Anah screamed. He ran at the pudding, reached his hand in, and grabbed a chunk of it before rushing back to Cheese.

The wrath and animosity that roiled off the pudding at this diabolical stealing attack was palpable.

Snoop shoved the pudding under Cheese's nose, trying to push it into her mouth. She backed away quickly. "I'm not eating that!"

Snoop sighed in heavy exasperation, sounding almost like an adult. "You have to if we're going to get out of this. 'Sides, you love pudding, and this one's got heavy cream."

"It also wants to eat us," Cheese replied, voice tight and high with panic.

Anah noticed that there was a slight movement to the glob of pudding that Snoop had in his hands and she tasted acid. If she were Cheese, she didn't think that she could stomach it either. But then, to her surprise and disbelief, Cheese stuck her pink, pointed tongue out and licked at the pudding. Then she licked some more. A greedy, starved look plastered itself on her face as she began to devour the pudding, licking and licking and chomping and chomping in happy contentedness until Snoop's hand was so clean that you'd never know he'd just stolen a bit of dessert from a sentient sugar monster.

Cheese's tail twitched back and forth with languid pleasure as she licked her lips and began to clean her paw and bring it to her whiskers. And Snoop said, "Oh for the love of gods, Cheese, can you get to it?"

She snarled at him in frustration. "It doesn't work like that. I can't just make it come, you have to give it a little bit."

Snoop looked over his shoulder to where the booger ball had landed. It was now three quarters absorbed into the pudding, with only a hint of the soaked T-shirt bits poking out.

Anah was beginning to recognize his train of thought. She just didn't want to believe it because this was... this was insane. And yet it was an insanity that just might get them out alive. Gathering her nerves, Anah stood and went over to Cheese. She rubbed the girl's back, scratched behind her ears, doing all she knew how in order to relax the cat-girl's body. Anah hoped it would speed along the digestive process that they so desperately needed. Snoop smiled tentatively at her, realizing that Anah had picked up on his plan. So, he moved on to the last and most important part. "Stevie." he put his hands on the dragonling's shoulders.

With all the seriousness of a general leading his army into battle, Snoop declared, "You get to make fire."

She nodded at Stevie. "I can't, so you're gonna have to do it for me. Can you be my fire?"

Stevie's response was instantaneous. Their shoulders pulled back and they stood tall and proud. They moved as close to the pudding as they dared, while Snoop stayed beside them, helping to guide them and prepared to pull Stevie away should the pudding get any gloopy ideas.

Next to her, Cheese's face was beginning to contort with discomfort. She groaned, her cat claws kneaded her belly. "I think it's working."

Anah could have jumped with joy, even knowing what was to come. The horrendous fiery, smoky stink of it. At least the previous stinky disaster had prepared them for just such an event.

She had never been so happy to hear that someone had gas. She maneuvered Cheese over and said, "Let us know when you're ready."

Cheese sort of giggled, but turned and stuck her bum out, tail lifted high. The cat-girl kept peeking over her shoulders, making sure they weren't just going to shove her into the pudding, Anah thought. She groaned a bit more, clutched at her belly, then stretched.

"Oka, Stevie, are you ready?" she asked, sounding quite pained.

Stevie nodded.

"Fire away!" Snoop yelled out, sounding far too happy for the situation they were in.

It was... well, it was a fart. It was a Cheese fart. The lactose in the pudding combined with the sugar had managed to percolate and disrupt her digestive system in disproportionate ways. The gas that was expelled came loud and fierce. Stevie opened their mouth and coughed. No flame came out.

Snoop quickly reached under their nose and tickled.

"ACHOOOO!"

The fire from Stevie's mouth caught the heinous gas coming from Cheese and turned it into an actual fireball, much like the ones Anah liked to toss at monsters when she was out and about. The fireball not only hit the pudding, but it struck right where it needed to.

The booger ball caught. The oil that Snoop had soaked his T-shirt in lit up with such speed that there was a minor pop as it exploded within the pudding, creating a hole that was awful to look at because it was deep and dark and only led to more pudding.

Anah held her breath. Would it going to be enough? But the pudding managed to catch fire. It began to bubble. The skim of milk that happened when pudding was on the stove too long started to ripple and form and crack and reform all over its awful, shapeless body. It shrank. It hardened. It popped and groaned. And then it just sort of...

Burst.

There was pudding everywhere. It coated the front of her shirt. It had plastered Snoop and Cheese. Bucket was coated from head to toe. Through the door she saw Hailee had also been puddinged and looked pretty gross. Anah didn't want to know what she looked like. Enough of it was plastered to her to guess. She waited for the moment that the pudding came back to life, pulled itself together, and gobbled them up. It didn't come.

They waited some more. It seemed as if none of them could quite believe what had happened. But then, of all people, Bucket dragged a finger through the pudding covering his body, and stuck that finger into his mouth. He pulled it out with a slight pop. "It's overcooked."

# Chapter Twenty-Five

As soon as Pearl came tearing around the corner, her brown robes flapping at her sprint, Anah knew she had heard the explosion.

Miss Pearl slid to a stop. It was an actual slide, one in which she skidded, lost her balance, fell, and slid along the slick viscous remains on the temple's floor. She came to a stop near Hailee, who offered her a hand and helped pull her up. Anah noticed that Hailee didn't let go of Pearl once the acolyte was back on her feet.

"What?" Pearl surveyed the scene and asked again, "What? *What?*"

Hailee pulled the acolyte a little bit closer, throwing a strong arm around her shoulders. "Yeah, this one's going to be real hard to explain."

Pearl's gaze locked on with Anah's and they exchanged a sort of telepathic *oh you're going to explain* moment before Anah said, "Could we maybe get cleaned up first before we tell you what happened? Or do we need to get straight to that and cleanup comes later?"

The problem was the pudding was on Anah's skin. Textures had always been difficult for her, but this was overload. She could feel it. She could feel its cold, milky, goopy texture slipping and sliding on her flesh and it made her want to vomit. Every inch of her skin was crawling, which only made the sensations worse. This had to be one of the most god-awful moments in Anah's life, and she'd had a lot of god-awful moments.

For a heart's beat, it seemed like Pearl would deny her request. But then the acolyte sort of... gave up. Her shoulders sagged. Her head hung, blonde hair falling in lanky, pudding-drenched twists. "Yeah, fine. Whatever."

"Cool." Hailee, ever the articulate one.

"That sounds great," Bucket chimed in. He was still trapped by magic. Having hit a limit she hadn't known was there, Anah walked away. His pleas fell on ears too mucky to hear.

Pearl showed them to the temple's baths. There wasn't much, Dinna being a minor goddess. The temple was stunning but didn't have much for long-term patrons. Therefore the baths only had two miniature hot springs, one for the boys, one for the girls.

The others eagerly rushed ahead, but Stevie paused, looking back and forth between the two doorways. Anah immediately understood Stevie was in a hard place. One they didn't deserve to be in, because who was she or anyone else to tell Stevie which bathtub to get in. They were a *child*. Who the frick cared? Stevie was filthy. People should only care about getting pudding off. She went to the dragonling and held their hand.

"What if we just did one bathroom for the kids and one for the grownups?" she offered, carefully looking the dragonling over. She didn't want to hurt their feelings in her efforts to protect them, but honestly, she wasn't sure how she was supposed to handle this situation.

She must have handled it correctly, because Stevie relaxed and nodded happily. She looked at the other children. "Is that okay with you all?"

Cheese just shrugged. "All bodies are weird and kind of gross."

Anah agreed but kept it to herself.

Stump anxiously started in his thick voice, "But when boys and girls are together, that's how babies—"

Snoop slapped him upside the head, followed by another slap from Bruiser. "Ya have to be a lot older for babies to be made you, dummy," Snoop said before Bruiser patted his brother reassuringly on the shoulder.

Although Stump looked confused and chastened, he nodded. Accepting that they could go into the bath together and they would come out without any additional babies, he allowed himself to be led in. Anah shook her head, but she was stifling a laugh.

Cheese held Hope's hand, guiding her. After all, at this point they couldn't get much grosser, so who cared that Hope liked to dig in her nose? It was her digging that had helped save the day. After the children disappeared into the baths, Hailee, Anah, and Pearl waited outside a bit longer.

It grew tense, but Anah couldn't decipher just which parts were causing the strain.

"You can go into the other one as well," Pearl said, gesturing to the door leading to the other bathroom. It was generous, considering she was most likely going to have them tossed in a dungeon soon after.

"We just let a bunch of trouble makers into a bathroom by themselves." Anah crossed her arms over her chest, instantly regretting the move. She really was going to hork at any second. "We're gonna stay a little longer and make sure we haven't made a terrible mistake. If they roughhouse in there, they could get hurt."

Seconds ticked by, turning into what felt like minutes, before Pearl shook her head and said, "I just don't understand you."

That was a sentiment Anah could wholeheartedly agree with. She wasn't sure she understood herself anymore either. All the things that she'd believed before coming to the temple were now challenged. That she couldn't find real work because no one would trust her. That she couldn't be respected because she looked like a child. That she wasn't someone to be counted on or trusted or could do anything except go and fight the things that other people didn't want to, suddenly didn't seem so real.

Would the Wand of Birramos have made a difference?

Anah suspected it wouldn't help her where she actually needed it.

"That's probably fair." It was all she could manage. She was exhausted, covered in pudding, and had zero energy to tackle an existential crisis. Hailee patted her on the back, grimacing when her hand stuck to Anah's shirt, and pulling it away with a *fffwwwwick*. "You go ahead, I'll stay and then we can switch places." Anah had to accept that they were friends. Hailee knew Anah's idiosyncrasies was still with her regardless. She'd know just how uncomfortable Anah's body was starting to feel. Like the skin was shrinking and she needed to burst free of it or she might actually die. Relief flooded her system. "Thank you."

Within the marbled room—small but not so tiny as to remind her of the larder—there was a pool sunk into the middle. The water was steaming, the natural hot springs that were filtering into the temple feeding into the tub. Anah slowly pulled the clothes off of her body, having to pause every few minutes to take deep breaths and calm her nervous system. Eventually, when she was stripped, she moved to the water and stuck a toe in it. Never had a bath felt so good. She slipped into the water, watching the surface cloud over with all that was being washed away. She dunked her head under. When she rose out of the water, scrubbing her face, she relaxed against the side and just let herself be.

The soak wasn't just helpful for getting cleaned up. She could sense the tiniest reserve of magic reforming in her. The rest and relaxation that came out of being alone worked as a bandage akin to sleep. Anah stretched her feet out, wiggling her toes above the water, and could no longer hide from how scared she had been in the larder.

So many monsters, so many situations where she and Hailee and Bucket had faced down what promised to be certain death. And yet, she'd never before been paralyzed with terror. But in that larder, with that truly bizarre monster, Anah had felt a fear so deep, so primal, that it had shaken her to her very foundations.

She had been terrified for the kids.

Swishing back and forth, she moved her hands up and down her arms, even though she was already clean.

Anah had practically fallen apart over the possibility that those sweet, loving children might have gotten hurt and she couldn't do anything to stop it. That horror had drained her because the idea of a world without them in it had been too much to bear.

It came before she could stop it. The burning tightness in her throat that no amount of swallowing could erase. Her eyes grew blurry and overflowed before she could dash away the tears.

Anah sobbed, crying so hard that it ached. She cried until she was wrung-out and exhausted, her face puffy.

She got out and found a piece of linen that had been thoughtfully hung to wrap around herself, drying her gray skin, relishing the feel of absolutely no sugar sticking to its surface. She towel sponged her hair and put it back into braids. She even dried off her horns, eager to wax and polish them later. She had just survived a deadly dessert, and by golly, self-care was important.

She started to exit when instinct had her pausing. She peeked around the corner, not knowing what she would see. Would it be the children running around naked and crazed in the middle of the temple? Would it be the pudding come back to get them again?

It was Pearl and Hailee. They were kissing. It was the tentative awkward first kiss and was probably sweet, but Anah knew she'd only get caught up in how gross it was to swap fluids. She stepped back out of sight before loudly clearing her throat and coming back out again. This time, she found two adults standing painfully far away from each other, their faces red. "Your turn, Hailee. The water's amazing."

Her friend ducked and ran into the room, and Anah grinned. Then, feeling punchy, she turned to Pearl and said, "I thought you acolytes practiced celibacy."

Pearl looked shocked at first, then appalled. "Oh no!" she exclaimed. "I don't think I could get behind any deity that demanded celibacy. How awful."

"Good news for my friend." Anah winked.

The kids emerged before Pearl could respond. They were washed and dried and wrapped in linen towels just like her. While Anah felt relaxed, the kids seemed jubilant. They'd just defeated a monster, so they deserved it.

Pearl held out her hands, shushing them. "Well done, children. I'll have someone come pick up your clothes and clean them. As for now, will you please go with Miss Anah back to the classroom and don't set anything on fire, explode anything, make anything stink. Just go to the classroom."

They did, walking single file, following Anah through the twists and turns of the temple walls until they made their way back to the classroom. Everyone quietly took a seat, the aura of the room contemplative.

Once more, she recalled her fear and how they'd been braver than anyone could have guessed.

"I need to tell you something." At this point, having all of their attention on her no longer bothered Anah. "That was amazing. Each and every one of you were incredible and I'm so, so proud."

It was true. It had been amazing. And she was proud. The way that they'd worked together? That had been the sort of teamwork that seasoned adventuring groups could only dream of, and these were just kids. If they could keep up this type of camaraderie, they would be able to do whatever they wanted when they grew up. She almost felt bad for Farrow or whatever city they decided to take on in their adventures.

Instead of seeming pleased, though, they remained still. Tiny brows pressed together, and Anah grew wary of the somber atmosphere.

"How did he know you?" Snoop asked.

Anah looked at him sharply. "Who?"

"The halfling. He knew who you were, Miss Anah, and you knew him. How did you know him?"

Of course. Even in the apex of danger, Snoop never stopped observing. He'd witnessed and filed away everything she and Bucket had said, and was smart enough to know what it meant. Anah was busted.

No more half-truths would cut it, or white lies to gloss over the facts. It was time to confess.

"The halfling's name is Bucket. He stole from Hailee and me and ran here, to this temple. We came here to get back what was ours and to punish Bucket for betraying us." She inhaled deeply, steeling herself for the rest. "I put a spell on the temple so that he couldn't leave, but Hailee and I still needed a way to search and find him. He's very sneaky, and he's very good at hiding, so it wasn't something we would be able to do just in a day."

Understanding dawned on Snoop's face. It wrecked Anah. The others were a little bit slower to pick up on what was going on, but all of them, including Hope, came to the same realization that their gnome friend had.

"You didn't come here to be a teacher," Cheese pointed out, sounding a little heated, her tail flicking angrily back and forth.

"That was an accident. I honestly thought it was a terrible mistake. Pearl ran into us and mistook our reason for being here. She offered us a way in and we took it." She looked them over and the fondness within her was achingly sweet, which made the conversation so very sour. "I didn't like children. I've never taught a day in my life."

"No kidding." Cheese's wry tone hurt.

Anah might know magic but there were no magic words for this. She wished there were. "I'm glad it happened, though."

Snoop crossed his arms, sullen. "Because you got what you wanted? The halfling is still in the larder. You can go get him and leave, just like you planned."

Bucket was still in the larder, stuck fast by Anah's magic. He'd remain there until she'd accumulated enough power to release him. For once, Anah didn't feel particularly motivated to speed up the process.

She needed the time to make this right.

"I'm glad it happened because I got to meet all of you. Because I've had such a good time here."

Anah hoped the confession would be enough. In the recent past, whenever she had been open and vulnerable about her flaws and feelings, she had been rewarded. But this time it didn't seem to be the case. None of the children would look at her. They all slouched, and then slowly turned away, showing her their linen-clad backs.

It was as if she'd been stabbed. A painful evisceration where all of her good feelings bled out and she was left empty.

There was no wand, no magic, no luck that could salvage the hurt she'd caused. Anah had never felt so small.

# Chapter Twenty-Six

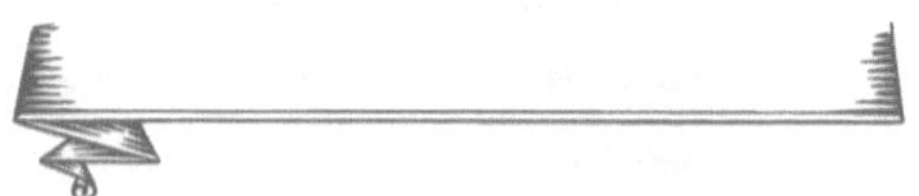

Poor Acolyte Thomas had been charged with watching after the children while Hailee and Anah were summoned to face Miss Pearl.

She waited, stone faced, in the hall near the larder. The stone was still tacky and the smell cloying. "Time to explain, please. What in Dinna's grace was that thing?"

"The missing pudding," Hailee offered.

Pearl scowled. "I suppose you think that's funny?"

"She's right." Anah pointed to some of the larger piles of goo. "The pudding that went missing apparently had a life of its own. I think it's been eating things from around the temple. It got large enough to attack us."

Pearl shook her head, refusing this explanation. "Desserts don't just come alive. I mean... how?"

"I wish I knew," Anah said seriously. That was the one thing she couldn't make sense of.

"Poor excuse for a monster aside, what about you. Who are you? Why are you here?"

Hailee shifted uncomfortably on her feet. Anah knew she was probably unbalanced and didn't know how to fix it. That was something they shared. Anah would bear her own loss and punishment, but the thought of Hailee being dragged down with her was a heavy burden.

"The halfling in the larder is a rogue named Bucket. He's been a companion of ours for many years. We're a band of adventurers, like I said before. But he's the reason we came to the temple. He stole from us, and I wanted revenge."

Pearl shut her eyes, looking pained. When she opened them, the blue of her irises had grown icy. "So you weren't answering my advertisements?"

"No."

"And when I figured out you weren't seasoned teachers, you decided to keep up the lie that you wanted to be here." Pearl wasn't asking a question.

"Yes."

Hailee swallowed a painful sound.

"You listened to me complain about being stretched thin. You brought trouble to the temple, putting the crèche in jeopardy. You let the children put themselves in danger over and over again. And when I was agonizing over things going missing, you knew who was causing it and you lied to me anyway."

"Yes."

Pearl trembled. Anah suspected the acolyte was working hard to contain her rage. "I'm so... so...*furious.*"

This time, Hailee whimpered, and Anah reached out to reassure her. Hailee flinched away.

"You should be." Anah heaved a sigh. "I was so focused on getting what I thought I needed that I put everyone in danger. I've screwed up, and however you see fit to punish me, I accept it. Just don't take it out on Hailee. She was really good with the kids."

Silence descended. Hailee was looking back and forth between the two while Anah waited for Pearl's judgment. She could already see the manacles and dungeons, her reputation ruined. After this, she'd never be more than an untrustworthy fell-touched who turned everything around her to ash.

When the silence stretched on, though, Anah grew antsy. She was deserving of all that was coming for her, so why wasn't it coming?

From the larder, Bucket called out, "Do I get to tell my side of the story?"

All three women snapped "NO" at the same time.

"Here's what's going to happen." Pearl began to pace. "You'll fetch water and soap. You're going to clean every inch of that... thing. If you figure out what caused it, I would be grateful to know so we don't have any unsavory sweets in the future."

"We can do that."

"Further, you're going to get your halfling out and make sure he stays out."

Anah waited for their own expulsion, or the part where Pearl listed all the awful things planned for them. "And then?"

"And then... I'm not decided yet." Pearl's throat bobbed and Anah saw the acolyte was fighting back tears. "I'm hurt and I'm angry. I don't want to make decisions until I feel less volatile."

That was remarkably fair and nicer than Anah deserved. "We'll get to cleaning, then."

"All of it," Pearl warned.

It took several trips to get enough water to begin scrubbing. It seemed like every time they wiped parts up, the rags became too saturated with nasty. Then they'd soak, rinse, wring, soak, squeeze, and get another small portion finished before the rag was too filthy again.

Anah's back and arms were killing her. She probably should have started Hailee's physical fitness routine years ago, because her weakness was apparent now.

Eventually they had to go into the larder and face Bucket.

He was a mess, slumped over in defeat.

"Anah," he rasped. "Will you please let me go?"

"Working up to it." Anah sat in front of him. Hailee sprawled out beside her. "You ready for a deep heart to heart?"

Bucket chortled and tried to lift up enough to see them. "Sure. Why not? I'm being punished. Why not add some deep, emotional talk to it as well? Especially as feelings are your forte, Anah."

She couldn't decide if he was mocking her or not. It didn't matter, since he was the one magically bound and she could up and leave whenever she wished.

"Why'd you do it?"

"It would be easier to tell you if I wasn't stuck."

"I guess that's a trial you'll need to overcome." But, softening, she said, "I'll have enough magic restored soon, I think."

Bucket stretched as best he could. "I'd been planning it ever since that last job. I saw the wand and knew it would be perfect. Gods, if you knew how nervous I was up until I snuck away. I spent days thinking I'd spew and you'd figure out what was up."

"I didn't have reason to doubt you," Anah answered. "It was a shock to wake up and find you gone."

He grinned, but it was a broken smile. "I should have planned it better."

"So you wouldn't have ended up trapped in a temple?"

"No. Well, yes. But, no." His cherubic features were earnest. "So you wouldn't have worried so much."

Worried? He thought she'd been... worried?

"Come again?" she asked, shooting a look at Hailee like *can you believe this guy?*

"You were so worried about me that you came here to try and save me. That blasted pudding made it impossible for me to get word to you, though. It was relentless, and I didn't want to lead it to the children."

"You did lead it to the children," Hailee said flatly.

"Why would I think they were in a larder? Also, who includes children in their traps? You could have trapped the amorphous pudding without them there. And preferably without snagging me as well."

Anah leaned back, head spinning. "You think we came here to save you and that the trap was for the pudding?"

A crack formed in Bucket's veneer. "Yes?"

"Oh boy," Hailee muttered. "You've stepped in it now, buster."

He looked utterly baffled. Anah was too tired for games.

"You stole from us, ran away from us, and hid in a temple of all places, forcing us to take on jobs as teachers to try and flush you out. I put the spell on the temple to keep you in, but I had no idea how much endurance you'd have for skulking about."

Bucket's jaw dropped open. "Steal from you? I just borrowed it."

"You 'borrowed' the Wand of Birramos and some jewels? *Why?*" Anah wondered if she'd slipped in the pudding and cracked her head. Maybe this was a hallucination.

"That stick with a hunk on it was a wand? I thought someone was playing a joke."

"It was no joke." Anah's teeth ached and she tried to relax her jaw.

"I knew the hunk was a fell stone. I borrowed it so I could get it cut and set."

Anah blinked a few times. Hailee wrinkled her nose. "Why?"

That earned Hailee a stinging glare. "Because of the *thing* we *talked about*," Bucket said through clenched teeth. "The *thing* I asked your advice on?"

This was... Anah wasn't sure what this was. Hailee looked dumbstruck. But then her eyebrows lifted and shock lit up her eyes. "My advice was not to!"

"I just thought you didn't appreciate my vision!"

Anah had the distinct feeling of being a third wheel hearing inside jokes she wasn't a part of. "Could either of you please just tell me what's happening? I'm about to lose my cool."

Her friends exchanged another private look. Bucket seemed to grow smaller. "I was going to get it turned into a ring. But I didn't have enough on me for the jeweler. So I came to the temple to get at my stash—"

"You have a stash here?" Hailee blurted out. "Since when?"

Bucket shrugged. "Since forever. I have stashes at several of Dinna's temples. That's why I always say I'm coming here to make change. It's a joke, but also I have money."

Anah briefly pictured burning everyone in the room, including herself, to a crisp. "Why a ring? What would you even do with a fell stone? You're a halfling!"

Bucket's cheeks changed color, shifting from petal pink to a raging scarlet. "I was going to give it to you."

"You were going to give it to me."

Hailee looked everywhere in the larder but at the two of them.

Bucket nodded quickly. "Yes. As a present."

Was she incredibly stupid? Why was everything suddenly so *weird*? Couldn't she just understand social cues for once in her life so she wouldn't have to scramble so hard to understand what wasn't being said?

"Why would you give me a present?"

It was Hailee, exasperated, who shouted, "He wants to ask you to marry him! Gods, Anah!"

Anah blinked. She looked at Hailee, then at Bucket. Her heart didn't want to cooperate , starting and stopping and lurching in a mash. "You were going to ask me to marry you?"

Bucket pressed his face to the floor like he was hiding. His answer came out muffled. "Yes. I love you. I thought... I dunno... I thought you felt the same way."

"But why would you think that?" Anah was tearing through her memories, trying to figure out what she'd said or done to give Bucket the idea that she loved him.

"You're nice to me and you're not nice to anyone."

"I'm nice to Hailee."

"But you guys have that whole best-friends-platonic vibe. I thought it was different with me."

Her swallow was painful. "I mean, it is different. And I do like—love—you both. But not in that way. I've just never been interested in that kind of love. Not when it includes all the touching and fluids. I just like being with the two of you. I love feeling understood. I always feel safe with you because I know that no matter how strange I am, or if I react the wrong way, you get it. Except now I'm second-guessing that." A thought occurred. "And I'm terrified my reaction to this is, uh, not the right one."

None of them seemed to know what to do. Hailee began to half-heartedly scrub some pudding.

Finally, Bucket fell back to the ground. "I'm so stupid."

Anah couldn't help the laugh. "Apparently, I am, too."

"I want to be stupid, too!" Hailee exclaimed.

"Can we clean this up and get out of here?" Anah asked. "I don't think I can handle anything else."

Agreed, she went ahead and pulled at her reserves once more. Her body was well and thoroughly pissed off at her and a crash was imminent. With a touch, she unlocked Bucket from the binding circle.

He stood and stretched, his knees cracking loudly. Then Bucket went to hug Anah, who scurried back in horror.

Hurt skated over his face. "Oh. I get it. I can do the platonic thing, you know. You're just cute and a very convenient height. I thought... but it's just going to be weird. That's okay. I'll handle it."

Anah held up her hands to slow him down. "No, we can be all that. But you're still covered in pudding and if it touches me again I will literally peel my skin off and set it on fire."

# Chapter Twenty-Seven

The hall and larder were clean. As were the children and grownups. As means of atonement, Bucket ventured back into the tunnels to try and find all the items the pudding had devoured.

Some he found, ruined by their occupancy inside an all-devouring dessert. Other items remained missing. Like the book on the Underhill gnomes. Acolyte Thomas made it clear just how happy he was to hear that—not very—and forbade the children from taking items out of the library. However, he acquiesced to them coming to the library and reading under supervision. Which, in all honesty, was probably for the best.

Bucket waited with Anah outside the classroom while Hailee said her goodbyes. Each exclamation of sadness that made its way to Anah hurt. Bucket patted her back. "I'm sorry. Surprised that you care, but sorry nonetheless."

Embarrassed to be so obvious, Anah aimed for indifference. "It's fine. I just spent three days with literal snot-nosed kids. I'm more than ready to find a real job after this. One that doesn't involve babysitting."

Her friend kindly said nothing because it was obvious to both of them that Anah was full of hot air. It had been three days, but that was ample time for the walls she'd built within to be dismantled, for emotions to sneak their tendrils in and take root, leaving her confused and wanting. Wanting for what, exactly, she couldn't be sure.

Pearl slipped out of the classroom to join them.

"Well." She looked as if there was more to say but she wasn't sure what it was.

"Thanks for not calling the guard on us." Anah swallowed hard. "That was more generous than we deserved."

Pearl only stared her down. Anah's petite size didn't help her avoid that particular steadfast gaze.

"Bucket, would you kindly let me have a private word with Anah?"

Anah grew hot. "No, it's okay. He can hear whatever it is you need to say."

In truth, she wasn't sure she could handle one more lecture alone. It wasn't as if Perl would say anything Anah hadn't already considered. She'd spent the entire night before tearing herself apart for every bad choice and dreading this morning's return to the temple. In the end, Anah learned she was her own harshest critic.

"I insist."

Bucket mouthed *I'm sorry* before slinking away.

Anah tried to ground herself for the onslaught. Instead, Pearl did something horrible.

She pulled Anah into a hug.

It was brief enough that Anah wasn't finished processing the action until it was over. She looked at Pearl quizzically. "I don't understand."

"I'm not sure I do, either. But I'd been praying for change for months before you showed up. The kids are wily and devious. No matter the credentials of the teachers, each and every one of them quit—the record is within an hour of starting.

"Perhaps Dinna listened, because everything has changed. I can't be angry simply because it wasn't the shift I wanted."

Anah would have called all of that religious horse crap, except she understood exactly what Pearl was talking about. Anah had entered the temple with change on the brain as well. As in, she was going to change Bucket's face by painfully rearranging his features once she had the wand. The only thing she thought she needed was more power.

"It did end up topsy-turvy." She longed for Hailee to hurry up so they could escape.

Pearl put a hand on Anah's shoulder. "I'll be thinking of you. Of both of you," she amended.

Anah grumbled. "Just don't think of me in the same way you do Hailee. I'm done with messy situations." She'd been serious, so when Pearl descended into snorting giggles, Anah found herself in uncharted territory. She really didn't want any more complications for a while.

"Will you be in Farrow for long?"

"Probably not. There isn't anything keeping us here." Anah struggled to keep the aloof façade going. How much longer would she have to endure this?

"I'm sorry. Perhaps it's best you didn't say goodbye to the children. After all, what would you even say to them?"

A fierce gust of protective love slammed into Anah. "Lots, actually."

"Like what?"

"I'd tell Hope that she's smarter than she thinks. She's six and still learning—not knowing something isn't the same as being stupid. And I'd tell the twins that I know what it's like for people to expect you to do one thing, but they don't have to be warriors. If they want to explore other opportunities they should, regardless of what people think."

Anah sniffled, picturing each sweet face as she spoke. "I'd tell Cheese to lay off the dairy but to keep her loyalty—she can be counted on in the most harrowing of situations and that's valuable. For Stevie... that their flames are a friend, not an enemy. But any friendship has trials and upsets, and its pushing through that strengthens the bond. Also to keep pursuing allergies, because their sneezing isn't normal."

Pearl laughed at this, pressing her fingers to her mouth like she wanted to catch the sounds before they escaped. "What about Snoop Dug?"

Anah tucked into herself. This was the one that hurt the most, she thought. "That he doesn't need to try and be someone big or powerful, because those things won't make him a better person. That he's wonderful and perfect the way he is. And that I know how much it hurts to be let down, but not to let that stop him from trying."

"Hmm." Pearl's hand dropped. "I wish they'd let you tell them that."

"I messed it up and broke the trust. Just let them know they can keep the spices—those were a gift."

"I'll do that."

Hailee finally met them in the hall, with flushed cheeks and red eyes. She and Pearl shared a look Anah didn't need help understanding. Instead, she left to find Bucket.

After, they made their way to the inn. Marcus was surprised to see Bucket—in one piece, specifically—but adapted quickly and made room for the halfling. Hailee immediately sat at the counter and ordered an ale. Bucket pulled up beside her, ordering the same, as well as several dishes of food.

"What? I've been living on scraps."

Marcus wrinkled his brow at that but tipped his head. "But if you eat all that you won't have room for dessert. The old lady's made an incredible custard, if I do say so myself."

Bucket and Hailee turned green, and Anah's stomach heaved. As she left to go upstairs, she heard Bucket's declaration of "Give me savory or give me death!"

In the room, Anah stripped to her underclothes and lay on top of the sheets. The heat of the day was at its peak and Anah wished she had enough magic to create a breeze in the room. At least now there was no reason she couldn't rest and recuperate. Hailee had offered to buy her some fell water but Anah thought it might draw unwanted attention as the stall had recently been robbed.

When she slept, it was dreamless.

BREAKFAST WAS A MOROSE affair. None of them knew what to say to each other. It was as if they'd wrung out every intimate secret from themselves until there was nothing left to give.

Just to hear something other than her self-berating thoughts, Anah asked Bucket, "Why Dinna's temple?"

Through a mouthful of food, he said, "Because I'll never grow and probably won't change, so her halls were the perfect place to store items. No one would think to look there." He chewed thoughtfully. "But then I couldn't get out, and I'll admit it deflated my ego. You did that? How?"

"I had some of your hair. From there I combined a containment spell with a tracking spell, so that the containment only pertained to you, regardless of where you were in the temple. After that, it was a matter of flushing you out."

Bucket tipped his head in acknowledgment. "You'd have been waiting a long time were it not for the pudding."

All three sat with this. Yes, there were misunderstandings and knee-jerk reactions, assumptions and unchecked impulses that had landed them where they were. But the pudding remained the unexplained variable and was going to haunt her.

"I just wish it hadn't eaten the Wand of Birramos," she bemoaned.

"You still want it?" Hailee looked skeptical. "After all that?"

Anah tore her bread into tiny bits to give her hands something to do. "It would be nice, not necessary. But even without being cut to shape and attuned to a cambion, it's still a wand. Did the thing digest? Is it just sitting somewhere in the tunnels?"

Bucket slowly chewed, brow furrowed. He swallowed hard. "It did digest things. That's how I found it. I was in the vents and found coins, but they were sticky and tarnished. After that, the skeletons of mice and rats, bare-boned and smothered in vanilla." He made a gagging noise. "I knew something was in there with me, and I was trapped." Bucket looked pointedly at Anah.

"I'm not apologizing. I don't know how you thought I'd react to you running off, but it wasn't grounded in reality."

"I'd hoped Hailee would stall. Since we talked about it." He turned his ire to the monk.

"Nuh-uh. Not pinning it on me, dude. You said, 'I'm going to ask Anah to marry me' and I said, 'that's a terrible idea' and you said, 'all I need is something special to show her how I feel' and I said, 'it won't matter, Anah's aromantic and might set you on fire.'"

"You didn't say she was aromantic!" His cheeks were red. "You said 'good luck'!"

Hailee tilted her head, thinking. "Maybe I just said the aromantic bit in my head. But how could you miss the sarcasm in my 'good luck'?"

Anah hit the table, the stoneware rattling. "Hashing it out like this helps no one. Let's stay on the pudding."

"I've heard of jelly-like creatures that are squarish and absorb things to break down with acid," Bucket offered. "But this thing moved. I followed the trail—it was nasty, let me tell you—and found it in the classroom. It was devouring those poor kids' things. So I shouted at it, which was dumb, because then it chased me. I'd been scrabbling away for hours, disoriented and thirsty, hot and sweaty."

"And in all your following it, you never saw the wand? Is it possible it went places you didn't?" Anah's stomach shifted, unsettled.

"I don't think so. I followed the tracks and it didn't go anywhere without leaving something gross behind."

"When was the last time you had the wand?" Hailee grabbed a new hunk of brown bread and smeared it with butter.

"Oh, that's easy. I was in the kitchen when I heard those kids coming. The teacher, Pearl, followed and was yelling. I watched from a hiding spot under a table. But then Pearl threatened to get the guard and I didn't know if she meant for the kids or me. When she stepped out, I hurried back into the vent system. But there was flour on the floor and I had to put down the wand so I could brush off my feet. I didn't want to lead anyone right to me. Voices came again and I panicked, sneaking back in and leaving the wand on the table. When I came back for it, the wand was gone."

It was strange to hear the events from his point of view. Anah shut her eyes, making the scene come to life in her mind. She spoke slowly. "That was Pearl, hiring us. Then we were in the room for a short time before Stevie set things on fire—"

Hailee, getting into it, added, "We realized Snoop and Cheese were missing—"

"You found them in the kitchen—"

Oh, Anah did not like the dots that were connecting.

"Snoop was on a table, stirring the pudding." Hailee gasped. "But all the dishes were dirty."

"And my boy Snoop is fastidious about his food. He would have used whatever was nearby to stir."

"Hold up, hold up, hold up," Bucket interrupted with a small shake of his head. "Are you saying that hunk of rock on a stick brought *life* to the pudding?"

Anah cringed, hearing how it sounded. But the explanation lined up. "Yes?"

"And it could do that *before* your plans to make it mega powerful?"

"...yes."

"Anah, it's still in the temple kitchen. It has to be."

Hailee waved this away. "No way. We scrubbed the place, remember?"

Anah's insides threatened to drop out and through the floor. "It's with the kids. Kids that have notoriously sticky fingers, remember? We have to go back."

"Pearl won't be happy to see us," Bucket said. "Well, she'll probably be glad to see Hailee, but you and me? Not so much."

"She'll be even more pissed if the kids use that wand and something worse than pudding happens." Anah was already moving.

They attempted to race through the streets, but the market was so crowded and loud that they were constantly in danger of being separated. Finally, Anah cast dignity aside and had Hailee scoop her and Bucket up, one under each arm.

It was uncomfortable and humiliating, and Anah would have endured a thousand times worse if it meant saving those kids.

Hailee bounded up the temple steps before setting them down. She opened the mammoth, carved wooden doors.

They rushed past patrons, disturbing silent prayers. When they got to the door to the inner sanctum, Anah stopped. Her heart punched against her ribs from sprinting.

"What are you waiting for?" Hailee demanded.

"The wards. Pearl had to have warded against us."

"Bucket, how did you get in?" Hailee was frantically searching for some small hole or crevice they could use.

"It's way at the back—"

Anah took a deep breath. She'd done so much wrong. But this was something she knew needed to be right. It had to be, because the stakes were too high. "I'm going in."

"But you said—" Bucket tried and failed to catch her wrist. Anah was already pushing in.

The wards glowed just like that first day. The scent of the magic activating burned in Anah's nose. But she was fine—and inside. "Come on!" She didn't wait, hurrying to the classroom.

Anah burst through the door, her friends pushing in just behind her. Sweat dripped down her temple and each inhalation was a jagged rasp. She bent in half to brace herself on her knee, dots popping up in her vision.

*A hundred percent asking for Hailee's help after this.*

Pearl stood, hands on hips, her eyebrow cocked. "Yes?"

Anah wanted to speak, but she needed oxygen more. She held up a finger, gulping in air.

"Of course," Pearl said, so dry the humidity of the day ran from her tone. "On your time."

The children snickered. Anah risked a peek at them despite knowing it was a masochistic action. Yet they weren't growling at her or turning away. All of them were laughing at her, yes, but it wasn't mean-spirited.

Stump cried out, "This is why Miss Hailee added in the exercise!"

"Yeah!" Bruiser agreed. "So Miss Anah could get fit!"

Snoop smirked. "She needs all the help she can get."

Tears pricked in the corners of her eyes. But Anah couldn't be sidetracked. Not yet. She straightened with effort, her side cramping. "I have something I need to ask. Children, it is imperative you answer honestly. While cleaning, did any of you find a wand?"

Confusion danced through the children, their chatter increasing in pitch and speed. Hailee clapped her hands twice, the sound sharp, and damned if every small spine straightened while mouths shut tight. "It wouldn't look like much," Hailee added. "Like a stick from a tree attached to a crusty black rock."

Anah hadn't thought it looked *that* absurd, though in hindsight she hadn't cared much about the looks at all, only what it could do for her.

Before more explanation was needed, though, Snoop raised his hand. "I used it—"

"We know," Anah said hurriedly. Pearl had been quite forgiving, but there was no point in risking him getting in trouble for something he couldn't have helped.

"Did you take it after that?"

"No, Miss Anah. I promise."

Pearl moved close, peering down carefully. "Are you sure, Snoop? He's telling the truth," she said firmly. "Anyone else? Cheese, maybe?"

"Mmmm not me," the cat-girl purred.

"Stevie? Hope?"

Both shook their heads.

All eyes moved to the twins. Who, despite their sweetness and the impression that they sometimes shared the same, singular brain cell, were practically dripping with guilt.

They shared a resigned look. Stump stood, saying, "I'll get it," while Bruiser only muttered sadly, "It was perfect for dress up."

Stump slunk back. He dropped the stone into Anah's open hand. For a moment, she couldn't breathe and it had nothing to do with fitness. She'd let it go, and yet the stone was hers.

"But where's the wand?"

Bruiser grumbled, "We threw the stick away." He glared balefully at the stone in Anah's hand, and her first impulse was to buy the twins some costume jewelry.

This, of course, was followed by the sinking understanding that she wouldn't be allowed back to give them anything.

Pearl cleared her throat. "Is that all?"

But Snoop clapped excitedly. "Miss Anah's got a fell stone! She's gonna be crazy powerful now! Maybe we won't have to clean or nothin', she can just whoosh it all up."

Anah clasped the stone tight to her chest, making sure her heart didn't burst out of her chest. She couldn't do that, but she wished more than anything that she'd have a chance to try.

"Sorry, buddy." Her voice cracked and she fought for control of herself. "We came for the stone. I don't want anyone getting hurt by accident. We better go now."

And then, in her biggest challenge yet, Anah did the impossible. She walked away before she could make things worse for everyone. Everyone but her, because she thought it might be possible this hurt would wound her beyond healing.

Just before they exited the temple, Anah heard a shout. "Wait!"

It was Pearl, jogging toward them. She came to a stop. "I need you to know something."

Certain this was for Hailee, Anah grabbed Bucket and made for the door.

"Anah, don't leave without hearing me out."

Surprise rendered Anah useless. She faced Pearl and waited, unsure of what was coming. The uncertainty was greater than her need for control. Besides... Hailee and Bucket were beside her. That would make it okay.

"Okay. Whatcha got?"

Pearl leaned back, startled, before collecting herself. "You passed through the wards?"

"Yes. I think they might be losing their mojo, though, since we've gone through twice and they allowed it." Anah took a deep breath. "If you'd like, I can help make them stronger after I recover some."

Pearl cocked her head. "What? Nonsense. They work exactly as they should."

Anah gestured to herself and her companions to suggest *clearly not*.

With a smile, Pearl said, "Remember what I said. They allow in anyone seeking Dinna's grace. Which is to say, in need of change and growth. That you were able to get through now . . . Maybe it's just me, but I think that might mean something."

"Something that *isn't* faulty wards?"

"Yes."

Anah stared. The fell stone was heavy in her fist. What did Pearl want from her? For her to leave? Or to, what, stay?

"Look, I'm not always great at understanding nuance. Are you asking us to come back?"

Pearl did this strange thing with her face that made the situation more undecipherable. "Of course, we can't have any non-guild workers in the crèche. I'll have to send yet another request to the babysitters' guild. And who knows who they'll send?" As she spoke, she winked a lot.

It was weird.

"Riiiiiight. Well. We'll be off."

They'd made it back to the Drunken Goat before Anah asked, "That was weird, right?"

"Totally weird," Hailee agreed.

Bucket, however, had his contemplative expression on and said nothing. It wasn't until dinner, when Anah was starting to spiral over her unknown future, that he spoke up.

"Are we going to find a new job?"

"Do you mean, like, tomorrow? Because I'm going to need more time to get over the girl," Hailee said quite morosely as she pulled into herself.

"Yeah. We need to recover." Anah figured they'd assume she meant magically. But she had a fell stone and, while it may not be as powerful as the wand as a whole might have been, she was certain it would count for something.

Bucket let out an exasperated sigh. "No, I mean, is that what we want to do? Because I'm already going to struggle with being just friends with the woman of my dreams." He blew a kiss to Anah, and she stuck her tongue out at him. "I'd rather not travel with two pouters, you know? If you're just going to be all grumpy and sad, I'd rather not."

"Wow." Hailee stretched up. "Coming in with the sweet words already, Bucket. I'm going to assume you've got an idea already? Let me guess. A new adventure. More gold. Fame and fortune. So rich we'll forget all about this."

Anah appreciated Hailee's wry response. She wasn't in a place where she could contemplate the next day, much less her future.

"Uh, no. This ties more into what Pearl was saying."

And so Bucket laid out his plan in detail. It was a simple idea, really, but a lot would be left up to luck.

While Anah normally despised plans that included chance, this one held potential. By the time they made it to bed, she'd not only agreed to Bucket's suggestion, but was eager to get started. It wasn't something she'd have come up with, but it was worth trying.

# Epilogue

To: Pearl, Acolyte of the Goddess, Temple of Dinna
 We regret to inform you that, due to internal reasons, our guild is no longer banded together. We are unable to fulfill your requests.

 Best of luck.

 The (Ex) Babysitters' Guild

 P.S. I've heard a rumor of a new guild forming at Farrow City Hall that may be of interest. Perhaps you could start there.

*To: Pearl, Acolyte of the Goddess, Temple of Dinna*

*Thank you for the inquiry into Farrow's guilds. I went to make a list of those guilds I thought relevant to your request, but there is only one. So, you know, short list. I've attached the names of the founding members. Hope this helps!*

*Dan, Farrow City Hall Peon*

*To: Pearl, Acolyte of the Goddess, Temple of Dinna*

*WE APPRECIATE YOU REACHING out, Miss Pearl. While only just formed, we feel certain our guild can provide the assistance you require. Because we're a real guild, and that was something you said was non-negotiable. So there's no doubt now, real guild, all authenticated by City Hall and everything. We even have a notarized parchment, in case you wish to verify.*

*When is a good time to interview?*

*Anah and Hailee, The Crèche Keeper's Guild*

Her request had finally been answered. Funny, Pearl mused, how she'd needed to change her expectations in order to receive aid.

"If you'll follow me through this door, I only have a few questions for you," she said, leading the way for the applicants. "Watch out for the wards."

"Thanks for the warning." Anah stepped through, Hailee following. Nothing happened but a mild pulse of magic as the wards registered the bodies. "Seems like we passed the first test."

"Yes, well, I think you might find that the easiest part of the job. Now, I have some questions for you—"

Pearl was cut off by a short shake of Anah's head. Anah's teasing attitude was gone, and Pearl could see she was all business.

"Actually, I have a question for you, Pearl." Instead of asking, though, Anah shared a fearful look with Hailee. Pearl wished she could make the small woman feel better, but Anah seemed to come into things at her own pace. Pearl suspected she'd need to spend much more time with Anah before she could parse out all that bubbled under her surface.

"Ask away."

"Do they know we're coming back? Do they even want me to?" Anah chewed on a lip before adding, "They were so mad at me."

"Hmm." Pearl didn't want to make light of Anah's concern. It spoke volumes of the growth in the woman that she'd even shown up. *Oh, Dinna. You sneaky goddess.* Change wasn't always what one wished for, but began with what one needed. Anah needed to know if she was wanted.

"I have a secret to tell you." Pearl folded her hands in front of her. "I set up a scrying mirror the day you left. When I came out to talk to you in the hall—"

Anah's crimson eyes widened. "—they were able to see it?"

"And hear it. So I can say with utmost honesty that yes, they know you're returning and they are desperate for it."

Anah didn't cry, but her lower lip wobbled. "Okay. But I have to warn you, things might get messy."

Laughing, Pearl turned to escort them to the classroom. She didn't need to ask questions, she already had all the necessary answers. "That tends to happen."

Just before going in, Pearl turned to Hailee. The woman's brown skin was smooth and rich, her long black hair pulled up in a bun. When Hailee caught Pearl staring, she winked. A rush of warmth moved through Pearl's veins and, for a second, she forgot why they were standing there.

Then an angry scream—it sounded like Hope—jerked her into the present.

"I'll see you after school?" she asked Hailee.

"For sure." Hailee elbowed Anah. "I'm totally hot for teacher."

Anah groaned. "And she's hot for you. How very nice. Can we get to it?"

The row in the classroom increased, and Pearl wondered where Acolyte Thomas was. Most likely crying in the bathroom. Dinna knew she'd had those days, too.

Straightening her back, Pearl stormed into the room with all the confidence of a woman prepared to *wreck some stuff*. All around the room, children froze.

Hope's face was red and snot was simply cascading from her nose. Thank goodness she wouldn't have to deal with it. That was all on Anah and Hailee.

Something moved behind Hope's back. Warning bells went off in Pearl. "What do you have?"

"Nuffin." The poor child was struggling to speak through her goo.

"Put it away before I take it away, do you understand?"

"Yes, Miss Pearl."

Pearl waited, sensing the anticipation grow thick around her. "Children, I'd like to introduce you to your new teachers. There are two of them, so you'll always have an eye on you."

Despite her scary teacher voice and stern face, the kids went wild when Anah and Pearl came in. Snoop ran straight into Anah's arms and refused to let go of her. Hailee and the twins were whooping loudly, and Hope jumped and clapped. Stevie started sneezing but managed to get a handle on it before things got fiery.

It turned out he was allergic to chalk dust. They'd switched chalk and slate out for charcoal and reusable parchment and there'd been only the random attack when something stirred up the room.

Something like, say, the chaotic cacophony happening at that exact moment.

Pearl did something she'd never done before. She didn't worry about it. She'd go to her office and catch up on paperwork. She'd meet with the elders.

And she wouldn't even scry to make sure things were okay, because she already knew that everything—and everyone—was exactly where they needed to be.

"IT'S JUST A STICK," Hope muttered angrily under her breath. Bruiser had threatened to break it, calling her a baby. But her blankie was gone, destroyed by the pudding. So she'd found a new object for her complete adoration and attachment.

It wasn't just a stick. It was *her* stick.

She wasn't going to tell any of them about it, either, because once they saw what it could do, they'd want it for themselves.

"Now... what can I bring to life?"

### *Authors' Notes*

We get mistaken for each other. Our cars are the same model, different colors. We experiment with our hair. We're best friends... So why not write together as well?

Oh sweet, sweet codependence.

It's been a ride. Many things were learned, or re-learned (like Ware's frustrating habit of waiting until the last minute for *everything*). Some tears, some sweat (it gets real hot here in the summer, y'all), and thankfully no blood.

### *Ware*

I SO RARELY WRITE FOR pleasure. My days are spent ghostwriting for others, or editing, or some combination of the two. Thanks to Faith for encouraging me to return to the stories that make me happy: the ones with fart jokes and puns. Thanks also to my family, who've tolerated me for so long. Huge thanks to prescription medication, which helps me manage my mental health and makes getting out of bed (sometimes with enthusiasm!) possible. To my mom, Joe, Max, and Leah. I've got the best family and I don't take it for granted. To Zack because I still like you after all this time. Crazy, I know. And to my daughter, E, who is the one who got really, really excited about a story where kids get to fight big, yucky blobs.

### *Faith*

BOOKS, LIKE CHILDREN, are best raised in community, but sometimes raising both at the same time is overwhelming. Huge thanks to J, for inviting me on this journey. To Ashley, Emily, and the rest of the crew who kept my kids safe and entertained. To Cara and Stacey for being the other half of the world's best Mommune. To Jen, Jo, and Eva, who fielded some of the most unhinged text messages, and my parents, who believed in my creative ambitions from day one. To Phoebe, Lucy, and Julian, for giving texture to some very long summer days. To Sandy, Cynthia, and Lisa, who's trust gave me the experience to know I don't want to be a full-time crèche keeper. To Nancy, who loved even when she didn't know who I was and left a rich heritage of sisterly love. To Chris, for not giving up on me even when I tried to. And to P & C, who inspire me to dream bigger every day. Being your mom is the greatest adventure of all.

Vintage Pixie Press publishes queer fiction. We aim to write what brings us joy, crossing genres and archetypes to share that delight with our readers. We write and publish our own projects as well as offer editing, beta reading, and virtual assistant services to other indie authors.

Vintage Pixie Press is operated on the traditional land of the Lumbee, Eno, Tutelo, Saponi, Occaneechi, and Shakori Native people.

www.ingramcontent.com/pod-product-compliance
Lightning Source LLC
Chambersburg PA
CBHW020108310726
48970CB00002B/531